ROMANCE OF PRINCE EUGÈNE

THE ROMANCE

OF

PRINCE EUGÈNE

BY

ALBERT PULITZER

Translated from the French

By MRS. B. M. SHERMAN

NEW YORK
DODD, MEAD AND COMPANY
1895

University Press:
JOHN WILSON AND SON, CAMBRIDGE, U. S. A.

PREFACE.

———◆———

POETS and novelists have dwelt fondly upon the
ecstasies of love, when sheltered under the eaves
of a cottage. If the shepherd's idyll merits the telling,
it seems to me that the one which flourishes under the
shadow of a throne is not the less worthy. And does
not the proverb say, "All the world loves a lover,
whether he be prince or pauper"?

By chance, glancing over the Memoirs and Correspondence of Prince Eugene, published, about forty years
ago, by A. du Casse, in ten octavo volumes, I read with
real pleasure the letters addressed by the Prince to his
wife, born Princess-Royal of Bavaria, and considered one
of the handsomest women of her time. These letters,
written during the stirring transformations of the Napo-
leonic epopee, reveal, in the exquisite tenderness which
they breathe, one of the most charming love-stories
which history has given us. On the eighth anniversary
of his marriage, the Prince thanks Heaven for having given him "the most beautiful, the best, and the
most virtuous of wives." This graceful and romantic
side of the Prince's character seemed to me worthy of
being shown to the world. But his letters to his wife

are intermingled with war news and interminable technical reports, which throw no light on the heart sufferings of this charming Princess, menaced with the loss of her heroic husband on the plains of Germany, in the gorges of the Tyrol, or the snows of Russia. I thought, in disentangling them from this chaos which is interesting, no doubt, to the historian, but fatiguing for one who is attracted to the lovable, poetical side of things in this life, that I should be performing an agreeable task for many people.

If, in presenting this charming idyll to my readers, I can touch some sensitive hearts and inspire them with a little of the sincere admiration which I myself felt for this ideal love-story, I shall be fully recompensed for my labour.

THE AUTHOR.

CONTENTS TO VOLUME I.

CHAPTER I.

PAGE

Prince Eugene's Childhood. — His Military Tastes. — Development of his Character. — His Precocity justifies his Military Career. — His Marriage. — The Princess of Bavaria and Napoleon I

CHAPTER II.

Mutual Affection of Husband and Wife. — Their Popularity in Italy. — Eugene as a Patron of Arts and Sciences. — Napoleon advises him to amuse himself more. — Admirable Results of his Administration. — Satisfaction of the Emperor. — He names Eugene Heir Presumptive to the Crown of Italy 39

CHAPTER III.

The Campaign of 1809. — Mobilisation of the Army of Italy under the Command of Eugene. — His Private Correspondence with the Princess. — Italy Invaded. — A Defeat. — Bulletins of Victory. — Pursuing the Enemy. — March upon Bruck. — Campaign in Hungary. — Eugene wins the Great Victory of Raab. — Triumphal Return to Italy 53

CHAPTER IV.

PAGE

Divorce. — Josephine's Resistance — Eugene's Intervention.
— His Admirable Disinterestedness. — The Empress at
Malmaison. — Relations between Josephine and Napoleon
after the Divorce. — Eugene and Hortense's Filial Devotion. — The Prince's Return to Milan. — Grave Consequences of the Divorce for Eugene 108

CHAPTER V.

Prince Eugene refuses the Throne of Sweden. — Family Life.
— Birth of the King of Rome. — Eugene is summoned by
Napoleon. — Rupture with the Czar. — The Crown of Po-
land. — Eugene resolves to refuse it, if it is offered to him.
— Prospects of Peace. — War is Declared 147

CHAPTER VI.

Campaign in Russia. — The Passage of the Niemen. — Suf-
ferings of the Army from the Commencement of the
Campaign. — Russian Tactics. — The Uneasiness of Ab-
sence. — Napoleon as the Father of a Family. — The
Battle of Moscow. — Prince Eugene's Glorious *Rôle* in
this battle. — Entry into Moscow. — Incendiarism. —
Uncertainty as to the Future. — Overtures towards Peace.
— The Order to Retreat 180

CHAPTER VII.

Retreat from Russia. — Misery and Sanguinary Combats.
— Smolensk. — The Beresina. — The Emperor leaves
the Army. — The Twenty-ninth Bulletin. — Last Proofs.
— Desertions. — Adieux to the Cossacks 216

CHAPTER VIII.

PAGE

Departure of King Murat. — Eugene as Commander-in-Chief
of the Grand Army. — Difficulties of the Situation. — The
Retreat on the Oder. — Discouragement of the Army. —
Efforts of the Prince to reorganise it. — The Retreat on
the Elbe. — Return of the Emperor. — Eugene at Lützen.
— Departure for Italy . . . .　251

LIST OF ILLUSTRATIONS.

VOL. I.

PAGE

PRINCE EUGÈNE, DUKE OF LEUCHTENBERG . . *Frontispiece.*
   After the original painting in the Castle of Arenenberg.

THE EMPRESS JOSEPHINE 4
   From the original painting by Gérard in the Louvre.

NAPOLEON 110
   From the original by F. Gérard.

PAULINE BONAPARTE 131
   After the painting by Robert Lefèbre.

MARIA LETIZIA RAMOLINO (MADAME BONAPARTE), MOTHER OF THE EMPEROR 144
   After the painting by F. Gérard.

MARIE ANNE ÉLISE BONAPARTE, GRAND DUCHESS OF TUSCANY. 200
   After the painting by R. Lethierie.

THE

ROMANCE OF PRINCE EUGENE.

CHAPTER I.

Prince Eugene's Childhood. — His Military Tastes. — Development of his Character. — His Precocity justifies his Military Career. — His Marriage. — The Princess of Bavaria and Napoleon.

I.

THE star of Love, Prince Eugene's guiding planet, shone even over his cradle. His mother, Josephine Tascher de la Pagerie (afterwards the celebrated Empress Josephine), had loved and wedded at an age when other young girls have not yet crossed the threshold of their convent schools. The blood of the Island of Martinique coursed through her veins. Eugene, in his memoirs (dictated two years before his death), says that she was hardly fourteen years old when she married the Vicomte de Beauharnais, who was later on the President of the Constituent Assembly.

At the time of Eugene's birth, September 3, 1781, the first symptoms of the Revolution had already manifested themselves; but few were thoughtful and attentive enough to the distant rumbling to take in the full gravity of the situation, or to gauge the violence of the ideas and passions fermenting in the hearts of the masses. M. de Beauharnais was among the first to comprehend the meaning of the signs. He espoused the popular cause with the greatest ardour and generosity. Elected member of the Constituent Assembly, he took his seat on the Left. He was not long in attaining great influence, and was shortly chosen President of the Assembly.

Eugene received his first impressions while still a child, living as he did in the midst of these stirring events. He recalls with great simplicity, in his memoirs, the incident of his being present at a session of the Constituent Assembly under very touching circumstances for a child. His father, the Vicomte, imbued with liberal principles and generously devoted to the progress and liberties of the people, was seated on the Left. His uncle, the Vicomte's elder brother, the Marquis François de Beauharnais, on the contrary, had remained faithful to the traditions of the old monarchy, and was seated on the Royalist side. Eugene, who often accompanied his father to the sessions of the Assembly, as a rule remained near the stove, which was placed exactly on the dividing line of the two parties; it sometimes happened that he held his father's hand in one of his, while with the other he affectionately pressed that of his uncle, forming a loving and living link between the two brothers, enemies through political differences. What a touching remembrance for a child of nine years!

II.

Several years later, in 1794, the Vicomte de Beauharnais, falling under suspicion at the ending of a badly directed campaign on the Rhine, was led to the scaffold. His son was, according to the ideas of the day, apprenticed to a miller, and his daughter Hortense, the future Queen of Holland, to a dressmaker. The Reign of Terror ended, Eugene and his sister, taken from this slavery, regained their social rank; the young man entering upon his military career under the auspices of Hoche, to whom he had been recommended by his unfortunate father. Nothing could have

pleased him better, for he felt the blood of a gen-
eration of soldiers coursing through his veins.
It was just at this time that an event took place
which at first threatened to narrow his tastes,
but afterwards served as a stepping-stone to his
highest ambitions. His mother, the Vicomtesse
de Beauharnais, married General Bonaparte in
1796, notwithstanding the violent opposition of
Eugene and Hortense, who, venerating their
father's memory, looked upon the union as an
outrage to their beloved dead.

Bonaparte nursed no bitterness towards the
son of his loved Josephine, and he took him with
him in his Italian campaign, after having bestowed
upon him the grade of sub-lieutenant of Hussars.
The young man from the first showed himself
worthy of his ancestors; he was wounded at
Roveredo, the day after his fifteenth birthday,
and conducted himself throughout the whole
campaign like an old soldier.

After Campo-Formio, the young officer was
given a mission by Bonaparte, tending to develop
his experience of men and to mature his judgment. He was sent as France's representative to
the new republic of the Ionian Islands, where
he was received with great enthusiasm. After-

The Empress Josephine.

wards, his stepfather, who had become his idol, took him with him into Egypt. During the whole of this arduous campaign, Eugene displayed numerous proofs of courage, endurance, and military talent. On one special occasion, he showed, in a peculiar manner, the precocious firmness and dignity of his character. Aide-de-camp to the Commander-in-Chief, it was his duty to ride beside his stepfather's carriage. One day he positively refused to escort in this manner a lady upon whom Napoleon was lavishing his attentions, and who rode beside him in the carriage. He recalled his mother's husband to his self-respect, and nobly upheld her dignity. This firm solicitude certainly spared Josephine many hours of bitterness, and strengthened the esteem in which his general held him. He returned to France with Bonaparte, was associated with him in the perils of his *coup d'état*, and was made Captain of light infantry in the Consular Guard.

Eugene, who at this time had not attained his eighteenth year, was a man in every respect. Josephine, who lavished her love upon him, was lost in admiration of his martial and manly aspect, his firm and dignified bearing, the matured reasoning powers of his mind, ripened by adventures and habit of command, under the trials of a campaign carried on under the scorching African sun.   The First Consul evinced the greatest attachment towards him, and reposed a confidence in him far beyond that justified by his age, but increased by the young man's courageous and prudent conduct in Egypt.   He often made him the confidant of his inmost thoughts, as well as of the anguish which the malicious reports of his wife's conduct caused him; for he adored her in spite of her erratic behaviour.   Eugene tells in his memoirs how he often had to accept the difficult task of soothing Bonaparte's resentment and quieting the rage storming in his heart.   He acquitted himself with a delicacy and skill rare in so young a man.   His conciliatory words calmed his stepfather's anguish, and prevented him more than once from breaking the chain which bound him to a still well-beloved spouse.

Joined to these solid qualities, Eugene possessed an amiable and loving character, which had gained for him before this period the warm affection of those who surrounded him.   Constant, who was his valet before becoming the Emperor's, sketched the following portrait of the future Viceroy, at this early stage of his career : —

" He was good, gay, amiable, full of life, generous ; and his open, frank physiognomy could truthfully be said to mirror his soul. How many kind acts has he not done during the course of his life, and at a time when to do them imposed sacrifices upon him ! "

Another witness of his private life, Mademoiselle Avrillon, Josephine's lady-in-waiting, thus expresses herself on the character of Eugene :

" He excelled in all athletic exercises, and danced beautifully. Good, frank, and simple in his manners, without arrogance, without haughtiness, he showed himself constantly affable to every one ; and though he was not devoid of sensibility, he was remarkable for his gaiety. Passionately fond of music, he sang divinely, especially Italian music, which was, in fact, preferred by the family."

III.

If Eugene was an expert and graceful dancer, he was no less a frank and loyal soldier. He was in love with his profession, and despised the life of sloth and intrigue which was led in the antechambers of the great. It was at his own request that Bonaparte gave him a commission in the Guards, and that he accompanied him, in 1800, to the new campaign in Italy. Eugene was among the first to set foot on the soil of the new Peninsula. Some of the soldiers, on reaching the summit of Saint-Bernard, conceived the daring project of sliding down the abrupt decline; he joined these foolhardy men, and rapidly descended the mountain side, as though he were possessed with a wild desire quickly to enter this beautiful country over which he was one day destined to rule.

The young captain took part in many of the engagements of that campaign, and distinguished himself anew by his generosity as well as by his courage. At Marengo, in the midst of a charge, a wounded enemy fell to the ground in front of his company, as they dashed forward at full charge. The unfortunate man raised his hands in supplication. Eugene perceived him, and gave the order: "Open ranks! protect this brave fellow!" His order was obeyed, and the wounded man saved.

This cavalry charge was so disastrous that out of the one hundred and fifteen horses which Eugene had in his company in the morning, but forty-five remained to him in the evening. His brilliant action won for him, at the age of nine-

teen years, the rank of Chief of Squadron. On
this occasion, Bonaparte wrote to Josephine:

"Your son is marching with rapid steps towards im-
mortality. He has covered himself with glory in all his
battles. He will eventually become one of the greatest
captains in Europe."

Returning to Paris, Eugene passed through
Geneva, where a series of *fêtes* was organised in
his honour. Madame de Staël, towards whom
Napoleon later showed so much aversion, composed some verses for this occasion, to celebrate
the glory of the French army and the brave
young officer, the city's guest. Reaching Paris,
he was delegated to carry the flags captured from
the Austrians to the Invalides; afterwards he
took part in the *fête* held in the Champs de Mars
in honour of the conquerors of Marengo. He was
greeted with the wildest enthusiasm by the populace. Eugene wrote these stirring lines on this
memorable occasion: "It was one of the proud-
est moments of my life." And he added words
which showed the modesty of his thoughts:
"These witnesses of esteem and public recognition seemed to me the best and sweetest recompense for our fatigues; they inspired me with a
noble pride and heartfelt emotion."

The young man spent the winter of 1801 in the capital. His cover was naturally laid at the First Consul's table, at Paris as well as at Malmaison; but, with his habitual delicacy, he refrained from taking undue advantage of this privilege. Constant has drawn an animated picture of the life then led in the Bonaparte household : —

"Society flocked there, but it was a heterogeneous society. Conversation never flagged ; games of hide-and-seek were organised; comedies were acted. Eugene was the life of these merry gatherings, at which Bonaparte found much amusement, without taking any very active part; and in everything he did, he showed to the greatest advantage."

The Duchesse d'Abrantès, who knew him intimately at that time, has left us a charming pen-portrait of him; which I cannot resist the desire to recall here, as it brings out the amiable and gracious sides of my hero's character : —

"His personality [she said] displayed an elegance much more attractive from the fact that it carried with it one thing rarely found in combination, — an unassuming frankness and gaiety. His laugh was that of a child's, but his hilarity was never called forth by an ill-timed jest. He was amiable, gracious, polished without being obsequious, a joker without being impertinent, —

a lost talent, let me remark in parenthesis. He was a good actor, a delightful singer, danced as his father had danced before him, who had earned the nickname of ‘ Beauharnais, the beautiful dancer,’ and, in a word, was a very agreeable young man.”

Is that not a delightful sketch of the man, and a proper explanation of the ardent friendships and warm affections which Eugene was capable of inspiring? He merited them, and, moreover, returned them with interest. Nothing could be more touching than the affection he displayed for his mother and his sister, except the devotion which he lavished on Bonaparte. He would not have hesitated to have sacrificed his life for that of his chief; and he proved it during the course of the winter.

One evening, going to Bonaparte’s house for dinner before repairing to the opera, he was astonished at the laughing greeting he received of, “ Well, you do not know, perhaps, that I am to be assassinated this evening at the opera? ” His stepfather’s features were so calm that Eugene at first looked upon his words as a jest; but he was quickly disabused, and was soon interested in planning how to defeat the conspiracy. He took a handful of his infantry with him, and preceding Bonaparte by about fifty feet, entered the Opera House as though he were the First Consul. At a given signal, the soldiers halted, Eugene retired, and the General entered his box. At the same moment the conspirators were arrested, without having an opportunity of using the pistols and poniards found upon their persons. A slight mistake in the carrying out of this plan, and Eugene would have received the death-blow intended for his beloved master.

IV.

The great love which Eugene bore for his stepfather did not prevent him, as already stated, from resisting him frankly. Like his mother, he was very much affected by the tragic fate of the Duc d'Enghien. The future Empress overwhelmed her illustrious spouse with bitter reproaches, to which he, who was ever ready with a prompt and quick reply, found not a word to say in extenuation. "Twenty years have passed since that event," Eugene wrote; and he added with an .emotion distinguishable through his simple words, "I was very much distressed, on account of the love and respect I bore the First Consul; it seemed to me that his glory was tarnished."

He also relates this touching incident: —

"The Prince de Condé, before dying, had expressed a wish that his little dog, to which he was fondly attached, should be sent — with certain other effects, which he desired to leave as legacies — to a lady, whose loving remembrances filled his last moments."

Eugene was very happy to learn that Josephine, a few days after the stormy scene with her husband, had found the means of complying with the last request of the unfortunate descendant of the Condés.

Eugene was made Colonel in 1802, and Brigadier-General in 1804, at the early age of twenty-two. Bonaparte himself did not reach this dignity until after he had passed his twenty-fourth year.

That same year Napoleon grasped the imperial crown, and Eugene suddenly found himself on the steps of a throne. Far from being filled with pride, he rather felt himself incommoded in his manner of living, and chilled in his tastes, by the minute etiquette of the new court. He was not impressed by the magnificence and the ceremonious pomp of the new life, but, in the superior trend of his mind, this very young man fled from

the honours so lavishly heaped upon him, preferring an active career to these empty titles. " I
was never struck," he wrote later, " nor dazzled
by these outward marks of grandeur." When
Napoleon offered him the post of Grand Chamberlain, he refused it, under pretext that his tastes
were altogether too military for any other career
than that of arms. " I must admit, however," he
said with a naïve and charming frankness, in later
retracing these years, " that if the Emperor had
offered me the post of Equerry, I might have
accepted it, because there were horses in the
question, of which I am passionately fond ; and,
besides, there was something in that post resem-
bling a regiment."

Shortly before the coronation, Eugene was
made Colonel-General of the Infantry of the
Army. He welcomed this promotion with the
greatest satisfaction, for the Emperor, to use his
own words, "left him in his element."

After this, cannot one be astonished at the
proud and loyal attitude he preserved, when it
was a question of regulating the succession to the
throne? Napoleon's brothers allowed their ambitious pretensions to be seen; they intrigued to
prevent the Emperor from adopting Hortense's

son. Eugene held himself aloof, an outsider to all competition. But his superior merit called forth a great deal of jealousy, and his enemies worked hard to excite distrust in his Emperor's mind against him. In January, 1805, it almost looked as though calumny had succeeded in these odious attempts; Eugene received orders to set out for Italy in twenty-four hours; and when he presented himself before Napoleon to make his adieux, the cold reception awarded him gave him to understand that he was really in disgrace. He set out, however, without a murmur, disdaining a justification.

Madame de Rémusat, in citing this incident in her memoirs, remarks that Hortense rejoiced greatly in this submission to Napoleon's orders by her brother. "If the Emperor," she said to me, "had exacted a similar obedience from one of his own, you would have seen rebellion and heard grumbling; but in this case, not one word of objection was spoken, and I think that Bonaparte will be impressed by this obedience." The Emperor, in fact, was so impressed, and especially by the malicious joy shown by his brothers and sisters. He had sent his step-son away in a moment of spleen, but, according to Madame de

Rémusat, "he wanted to immediately recompense him for the wrong done him."

V.

The recompense was not long in coming, and when it came was startling. Eugene had reached Tarare, and, on horseback, at the head of his regiment, under a heavy fall of snow, was preparing to march, when a courier handed him the following letter: —

TUILERIES, February 1st, 1805.

MY COUSIN, — I have named you Prince and Arch-Chancellor of State. I can add nothing to the sentiments expressed in the message which I sent to the Senate on this occasion, a copy of which I forward to you. In this you will see a proof of the tender love I bear you, and the hope I entertain that you will continue in the same path to profit by the examples and lessons which I have given you. This charge carries with it no obstacle to your military career. Your title is Prince Eugene de Beauharnais, Arch-Chancellor of the State, and you will be addressed as Serene Highness.

I pray God may hold you in His holy and loving care.

NAPOLEON.

Eugene hastened to reply: —

SIRE, — I have just this instant received the letter with which Your Majesty has deigned to honour me. I was already so overwhelmed with benefits that I thought it impossible to add anything to them. It has pleased you, however, to give me a new proof of your kindness in elevating me to the dignity of Arch-Chancellor of State and Prince. This dignity and title can add nothing to the boundless devotion and attachment which binds me to Your Majesty. These sentiments will end, Sire, only with my life.

Did this high distinction succeed in detracting from the natural modesty of our young hero? Not at all. He continued to live with his officers and men as formerly, and he remained impassive under the deluge of felicitations poured upon him, which he knew how to appreciate at their true value. The intoxication of pride had no power to move his heart. The only thing which really troubled him was the superb message addressed to the Senate by Napoleon, in which the latter raised an imperishable monument to the rare qualities of his step-son.

SENATORS, — We have named our step-son, Eugene de Beauharnais, Arch-Chancellor of State. No act in our power could be nearer our heart.

Brought up by our care and under our eyes since his childhood, he has made himself worthy of imitating, and, by the help of God, of surpassing one day the examples and lessons which have been given him.

Though still young, we consider him from to-day,

by the experience to which he has been subjected in the most important circumstances, as one of the props of our throne and one of the bravest defenders of our country.

In the midst of the cares and bitterness inseparable from the high rank in which we are placed, our heart has had need of the loving affection and tenderness of this child of our adoption, — a consolation necessary, doubtless, to all men, but more eminently so to us, whose every moment is devoted to the welfare of our people.

I pray that your paternal benediction will accompany this young Prince in every step of his career, and that, seconded by Providence, he shall be worthy of the approbation of posterity.

TUILERIES, February 1st, 1805.

On the 26th of May, Napoleon was crowned at Milan as the King of Italy. On June 5, he conferred the title of Viceroy on Eugene. This young man was not quite twenty-four years old when he became Napoleon's right-hand man, and the representative of his genius in the government of this brilliant kingdom.

Eugene accepted this new dignity in the spirit of a man, consecrating all his strength to the accomplishment of a heavy duty. He redoubled the ardour of his work to such an extent that the Emperor recommended him to take more repose and some distractions.

VI.

The labours of the energetic Viceroy were of
the greatest service to Napoleon in his campaign
in Austria in 1805. Owing to the foresight and
administrative talents of his step-son, the great
general found Italy prepared to defend herself,
and asking nothing better, after having already
repulsed the enemy, than to boldly attack him
on his own territory. But the Prince did not
content himself with contributing solely to the
Emperor's success; he desired to work for the
prosperity and happiness of the Italian nation at
the same time. Unfortunately, Napoleon looked
upon the kingdom as a country already conquered; for his war projects he had great and
incessant needs for money, men, horses, and military provisions, and he pitilessly imposed heavy
taxes on his subjects across the Alps.

When, on the one hand, Eugene desired to
forward the designs of the one to whom he owed
everything, and, on the other, endeavoured to
lighten the heavy duties imposed upon his subjects, it naturally followed that certain disagree-
ments arose between the Emperor and his Vice-

roy. These oftentimes aroused a discontent on the part of Napoleon, — a discontent which, to tell the truth, was but fleeting in its nature.

Napoleon, believing himself opposed in the slightest of his wishes, at once became imperious. For instance, Duroc, Grand Marshal of the Palace, holding his instructions certainly from the Emperor, in a letter to Eugene under date of July 31, 1805, at a time when the young kingdom was not yet two months old, accused him of over-stepping his powers and "doing things which belonged to the Master alone." To demonstrate to him more fully that he must always await orders from Napoleon, and execute them vigor-ously and to the letter, he makes use of the fol-lowing words, which go to prove to what a point the Emperor pushed matters when an obstacle, no matter how slight, was set up in opposition to his will : —

"To speak on the very smallest things, if you asked His Majesty his orders or his advice, as to changing the ceiling in your room, you must wait until you receive them; if Milan were on fire, and you demanded means of extinguishing the fire from him, you must let Milan burn, while awaiting his orders."

In dealing with a sensibility so touchy, the Prince needed to exercise a most delicate tact in

order to content Napoleon and at the same time
to gain the affection of his subjects. He succeeded marvellously in the one case as in the
other, but not without much trouble. The preparations for the campaign of 1806 augmented
still more the Emperor's demands on Italy. As
a careful and thoughtful ruler for the welfare of
his people, Eugene showed real repugnance to
aggravating the heavy taxes already supported by
the Italians. Napoleon scolded him, as can be
seen in a letter dated September 16, relative
to the requisition of horses and waggons, which
Eugene had found a trifle excessive. I cite this
letter, not for the importance of the fact, but
to show the kind of difficulties against which
Eugene had to struggle : —

"You have hired two hundred horses for General
Lacombe Saint-Michel. What are two hundred horses?
If the Austrians were masters of the kingdom, they
would not demean themselves by such economy. I
cannot see why you should feel such a repugnance;
and I am surprised the Minister of War has not enlightened you on the subject. In every similar circumstance, a requisition of horses has been made. It was
not nine hundred waggons I took when I was in Italy,
but two thousand, and these requisitions were made in
disorder, which was vexatious for the country. You

must not let yourself be frightened by the cries of the Italians; they are never content.   But force them to this reflection: 'What would the Austrians do under the same circumstances?' They would act with decision."

Eugene's reply was worthy of his rank, of the loftiness of his character, and of the watchful care with which he protected his subjects.   He wrote from Monza, his summer residence, and at the present day, that of the King of Italy:—

"If I have not earned the approbation of Your Majesty in the matter of certain refusals which I made to the French Army, I must certainly have explained my actions badly.   I take the liberty of forwarding to Your Majesty a copy of a letter from Marshal Masséna, and in it you will see that I gave him nearly everything he asked for.   General Lacombe Saint-Michel only received two hundred horses because he desired no more.   I only refused requisitions when there was a question of payment, and I always said to Marshals Jourdan and Masséna that I would furnish the army with everything in my power, but that I begged of them to accord to this country the conditions they would make with a Department of France."

Does not all this prove how anxious the young Prince was to economise the resources of the country which had been confided to his care?   In his place, some courtier, more occupied with trying to insinuate himself into the good graces of the Master than to strengthen the prosperity of his subjects, could easily have evaded these reproaches.

During the whole of the campaign, Eugene employed vigorous measures to maintain Italy, to guard her from attack on the part of the Austrians, and to prevent their sacking Venice. Napoleon acknowledged this on the battlefield of Austerlitz, saying to those who surrounded him: "Well, Messieurs, you see what Prince Eugene has done. I knew well to whom I had confided my sword in Italy!"

Such was the man. Good, intelligent, and brave, gifted with all the talents which make man superior, he showed himself worthy of the highest and most delicate functions at an age when the majority of men had but started out in life. We are now about to see him under a new aspect, — that of a faithful and tender husband, a loving and devoted father. He was, in fact, on the verge of a decisive period of his existence.

VII.

The Treaty of Presburg had made a kingdom of the Electorate of Bavaria, to which the Tyrol had been annexed.   Napoleon, returning from Vienna, stopped several days at Munich with his ally, Maximilian-Joseph, to whom he had just given a crown.   He was received with an indescribable enthusiasm, in which admiration for the victor of Marengo held a secondary place to the gratitude felt for the benefactor of Bavaria, so elated at finding herself elevated to the rank of a kingdom.

Napoleon restored numerous flags and cannons found by him in the Arsenal at Vienna, which had been taken by the Austrians sixty years before.   The Court and the people rivalled each other in the enthusiastic displays of their gratitude towards Napoleon.

Could they refuse anything to the author of so many benefits ?   And what he wanted for Eugene was nothing less than the hand of the Princess Royal of Bavaria, reputed to be the most beautiful, the most charming Princess in Germany.

Napoleon, as is well known, had a passion for making marriages. When it was a question of the welfare of Eugene, to whom he was attached by so tender an interest, he naturally looked for a connection which would be worthy of him and add to his happiness. His choice was an excellent one.

The Princess Augusta possessed a sweet and amiable character, and — which certainly did not detract from her charms — was of exceptional beauty. The following is a portrait which has been transmitted to us by a contemporary of this charming young girl: —

"There was an indescribable charm emanating from the personality of the Princess Augusta; she was not yet eighteen years old; she was tall, well formed, and of a sylph-like figure. Her natural dignity commanded respect at all times; her face was handsome rather than pretty, her complexion remarkable for its freshness, though perhaps too highly coloured. But what was most attractive in her was her sweet manner, which won the love and admiration of all who approached her. All these advantages were not hers by nature only. Education could claim the credit of a good share of them; she had been reared with extreme simplicity, and nothing could be more modest than her ordinary toilette."

This union was not definitely settled without some difficulty. The Princess was to have married

her cousin, Prince Charles of Baden, to whom
she was devotedly attached. The King of Bavaria, knowing there was no harder sacrifice to ask
of his daughter than that of relinquishing her
dearest hopes, lacked the courage, in the tenderness of his paternal love, of asking her to change
the course of her destiny so suddenly. Fifteen
days before she saw Eugene for the first time, the
King, though but a few steps separated from her
apartments, wrote her this touching appeal : —

"If there is the slightest ray of hope, my dearly
beloved Augusta, that you can ever marry Charles,
Prince of Baden, I beg you on my knees not to renounce
him; I should still less insist, my dear daughter, that
you should give your hand to the future King of Italy,
if this Crown was not to be guaranteed by all the
Powers at the conclusion of peace, and if I were not
sure of all the good qualities of Prince Eugene, and that
he was capable of making you happy. Remember, my
dear child, that you not only assure the happiness of
your father, but that of your brothers and the people of
Bavaria, who all so ardently desire this union. A proof
that this marriage is a desirable one lies in the fact that
the Baron de Thugut (Prime Minister of Austria) who,
unfortunately for our house, has retaken the governmental
helm, has commenced by offering the Emperor's eldest
daughter as wife to Prince Eugene. It grieves me to
wound your heart; but I count on the love and devotion

which you have always shown for your father, and the thought that you would not willingly embitter his last days.

"Remember, dear Augusta, that a refusal would make the Emperor as much our enemy as he is at present the friend of our house.

"Spare me the sorrow of an explanation which would be detrimental to my shattered health.

"Reply to me by writing or through your brother. Believe me, my dearest, that it causes me much pain to write to you in this manner; but circumstances which are more than imperious, and my duty to care for the interests of the country over which Providence has placed me as ruler, leave me no choice. God knows that I have only your welfare at heart, and that no one in the world loves you more than your faithful father and best friend."

Could the young Princess refuse to ratify the happiness of her family and people? That same day she sent these sadly resigned lines to the King, in which were revealed sentiments so exalted as to argue well for Eugene's happiness:—

MY VERY DEAR AND BELOVED FATHER,—I consent to break the word which binds me to Prince Charles of Baden, notwithstanding the pain it costs me, if by so doing I can guarantee peace of mind to a cherished father, and happiness to a people depending upon him.

If I put my faith in your hands, cruel though it may be, yet the pain is softened by the knowledge that I am sacrificed for the welfare of my father, my family, and my country. On her knees your child asks your blessing; it will help her to bear her sad fate with resignation.

VIII.

While his future was being thus settled, Eugene was in complete ignorance of what was passing at Munich. Only nine days after the Princess' consent, he received orders from Napoleon to prepare for the marriage. This order was as simple and formal as though it was a question of a manœuvre of troops on a battle-field:

MY COUSIN, — I have just arrived in Munich; I have arranged your marriage with the Princess Augusta. It has been publicly announced. This morning the Princess favoured me with a visit, and I conversed with her for a long time. She is very pretty. You will find her portrait accompanying this on a cup; but she is much better-looking.

I imagine that upon receipt of this peremptory order, Eugene must have experienced some uneasiness on the subject of his future. This woman to whom he was to be united for life was but a myth, upon which to build hopes of happiness, or suppress fears of coming misery for the rest of his life.

Three days later, Eugene received this second epistle, in the same strain as its predecessor: —

MY COUSIN, — Twelve hours after the receipt of this letter you will set out in all haste for Munich. Endeavour to reach here as soon as possible, so that you will find me. You will leave your troops in command of the general you consider the most trustworthy. It is not necessary for you to bring a large suite with you. Set out promptly and incog., as much to lessen danger as to prevent any unnecessary delays. Send me a courier to announce your arrival twenty-four hours in advance.

P. S. One hour after the receipt of this letter, send me a courier to announce the day upon which you think you can arrive.

Eugene set out several hours later. He not only hastened, as can be easily comprehended, to make the acquaintance of his *fiancée* in a more satisfactory manner than by means of a portrait on a cup, but he was also burning with impatience to see once more his mother, who he knew had gone to Munich to wait for him.

Eugene had hardly crossed the threshold of the royal palace in Munich before Napoleon sent for him, and, taking him into his private cabinet, advised him strongly to cut off his huge moustache, as he feared the fierce and military aspect of this ornament might make an unfavourable impression on the young Princess.

The first interview between the young people went far towards calming their mutual apprehensions. They agreed that there was nothing distasteful in the one for the other. Soon a mutual esteem and a full confidence in the future was established in their hearts.

As has already been seen from the King of Bavaria's letter to his daughter, Napoleon had given out that, in default of a direct heir, he would make Eugene King of Italy. The offer of an archduchess of Austria as a spouse for Eugene, to which the King had alluded in his letter, had confirmed his confidence in the high destiny reserved for Eugene. As Napoleon, already married ten years, was still childless, the Princess had every reason to hope that she would one day be Queen of Italy.

The marriage was celebrated the 14th of January, 1806, just eleven days after Napoleon had notified Eugene of his wishes.

I will not undertake here to recapitulate the pomps of the nuptial ceremony, which was performed in the royal chapel. All Munich was *en fête*. The city was profusely dressed with flags,

and was brilliantly illuminated in the evening.
On the façade of the Hôtel de Ville, under the
letters " A and E " in jets of fire, shone the words,
CORONA VIRTUTI, surrounded by allegorical tab-
leaux. All the municipal buildings, the palaces,
the monuments, the city gates, and especially the
Court of Honour of the Royal Palace, were fairy-
like. From sumptuous palace to modest cottage,
joy and gaiety pervaded all classes of society.
Munich thus evinced the enthusiasm excited
among her people by the alliance of the Royal
House of Wittelsbach with the Imperial House
of France.

The expression, " Imperial House of France,"
was a just one; for forty-eight hours after the
marriage, Napoleon recognised Eugene as his
adopted son. He gave him the name of Eugene
Napoleon of France. From that moment Napoleon, writing to Eugene, no longer called him
" My Cousin," but " My Son."

Joined to the affection which Napoleon felt for
Eugene, the esteem which the admirable qualities
of the young wife called forth soon sealed a close
and tender friendship between the Vice-Queen and
the Emperor. Napoleon, during the first years
of their marriage, wrote the Princess Augusta

several letters, which testified to the closeness of
this tie.   I will, before continuing my story, quote
a few of them.

Two days after the departure of the young
couple, he wrote them from Stuttgart: —

MY DAUGHTER, — The letter which I have just received from you is as charming as you are yourself.
The sentiments which I have confessed to you grow
stronger every day.   It is with pleasure that I recall all
your beautiful traits, and I feel the need of being assured
by yourself frequently that you are content in your new
life and happy with your husband.   In the midst of my
busy life, my greatest pleasure shall be the assurance
of my children's happiness.   Believe me when I say,
Augusta, that I love you as a father, and that I hope you
entertain for me all the tenderness of a daughter.   Take
care of yourself on your journey, as also in the new
climate to which you are going, by taking as much
repose as possible.   Remember you have passed through
much excitement this past month, and I am anxious
that you should not become ill.

I conclude, my dear daughter, sending you my
paternal blessing.

IX.

Baron Darnay draws an attractive picture of
the *fêtes* which welcomed Eugene and his wife
to Italy.   It can be thus seen that the joy of

the Italian people was equal to that of the King of Bavaria's subjects.

"The Viceroy and Queen [he writes], on leaving their carriage, found a delegation of twelve members of the nobility of Venice awaiting them on the shores of the first lagoon. They had accompanied the gondola set apart for the transportation of the royal couple, with the others destined for the officers of the Court. Two other gondolas of smaller dimensions followed in the suite. That of their Royal Highnesses was ornamented with all that oriental luxury could suggest. Silken stuffs, gold, silver, embroideries, plumes, were used in rare profusion; superb tapestries covered the tables and the chairs; flowers and perfumes were scattered everywhere. The gondoliers, dressed in gaily coloured silks, propelled this sumptuous vessel with majestic motion. The other two gondolas, equally enriched with silken hangings and ornaments, moved slowly along on either side of the first. Thousands of smaller boats, newly and beautifully decorated, circulated around these vessels; several carried musicians who filled the air with strains of triumphant music. These long and graceful gondolas, each manned with a dozen gondoliers and decorated with multi-coloured silks, shooting in and out swiftly and lightly; the noise of drums and cymbals, mingling with the roar of cannons; the exclamations of welcome and joy, — made the scene, during the passage of the royal couple to the palace, a never-to-be-forgotten one. . . .

"On their arrival at Milan, the Viceroy and Queen found their route bordered by troops in full regalia;

superb regiments of French and Italian cavalry stood in readiness to receive the royal couple, and extended far into the distance. Further on, the Guard of Honour and the Royal Guard shone in all the splendour of full dress, and regimental bands were placed here and there. The cannon's roar, mingled with that of church bells, elegant equipages, jewelled women, cavaliers, and an immense concourse of people in holiday attire filled the air with their cheers and greetings. Such was the homage and respect which surrounded the vice-regal couple's carriage to the Oriental Gate, through which they must pass to enter Milan."

As an example of Eugene's modesty and his aversion to everything approaching exaggerated adulation and flattery, Darnay cites a little incident which happened during these *fêtes*, in the course of a gala representation: —

"The interior of the stage represented Olympia, through which the illustrious couple were supposed to pass, presented to the public by two genii. At their appearance the actors prostrated themselves. The Viceroy was much hurt at such an attitude, and sent word by a chamberlain that such actions were reserved for a gracious Providence, and not for simple mortals."

Fifteen days later the Emperor sent advices to the Princess Augusta so paternally affectionate that you could hardly find a better proof of the deep impression which the refined nature and

charming personality of the new Vice-Queen had
made upon him, from the first moment he had
seen her: —

My Daughter, — It was with pleasure that I learned
of your arrival in Italy, and that you were well enough
to make the still longer journey to Venice without inter-
ruption. But what pleased me most was to learn from
your letter the assurance of your great happiness. I
take a real interest in your life, as you must surely know,
and I am not mistaken in hoping that you will be happy
with Eugene. Believe me, that had I not been convinced of this fact, I would from the moment of making
your acquaintance have sacrificed my political interests
to your welfare. Your letter, my dear Augusta, is filled
with those delicate sentiments which seem to belong to
you. I have ordered a little library for you. Perfect
your education by reading a great many good books.
I hope the Empress will send you the fashions, and that
you will tell me what I can send you to assure you that
I am always thinking of you, and what will be agreeable
to you and Eugene. Take good care of yourself: there
is a great deal of sickness here; I do not know if there
is much in Italy. In ending, my daughter, I recommend
my people and my soldiers to your care. Let your
purse always be open to the wives and children of the
latter. You can do nothing which will touch my heart
quicker than that.

I give you my blessing, my dear child.

It is only necessary to read the following lines
to see how enraptured was Napoleon with the

young couple, upon whom from the first days of their union no cloud, however slight, had come to disturb their perfect happiness.

Ten days after the foregoing letter he wrote:

MY DAUGHTER, — I sent you my portrait as a proof of my esteem and love. I received your last letter. I have listened with great pleasure to all the good things which have been said about you. I imagine that you have received your wedding presents before this; at the same time I sent you a little library. Tell Eugene how much I love him, and how happy I am to hear of your reciprocal happiness.

Receive my benediction, my dear child.

There is not a letter written by Napoleon to Eugene on strictest business, but in which some words of tenderness for his daughter-in-law are found. These expressions are often so intimate in their kindness as to be imbued with a loving meaning entirely their own. Such, for example, is this postscript to a letter in which he announces his arrival at Stuttgart: —

P. S.   Two kisses to the Princess Augusta, — one from me, the other from the Empress.

And this one from Paris: —

A thousand loving words to the Princess. I am glad to learn that she sustained the journey [into Italy] so well; tell her how much I love her.

Six months later, Napoleon, in his constant anxiety to see the women of France bear future soldiers for their country, wrote the following lines to Augusta: —

MY DAUGHTER, — I read your letter of the 10th of August with much pleasure, and I thank you for all the amiable wishes contained therein. You are right in counting implicitly on my sentiments; take care of yourself in your present condition, and try not to give us a girl. I will give you a recipe for that, though you may not believe me; "that is, to drink a little pure wine every day." Affairs are arranging themselves satisfactorily, and I hope to be able to send you in a few days instructions for your voyage with Eugene, which must be made slowly, in order not to fatigue you."

To this paternal, cordial letter, written in the grave style and amiable brevity of the Emperor, followed a fervent expression of maternal love. The following is a letter written by Josephine to her son, shortly after his marriage: —

"As your destiny becomes greater, my son, there is no necessity for your soul to become filled with pride. No matter to what height you may attain, I know that your sentiments are higher still. Such is the advantage a man has who makes his conscience paramount. In this you are the worthy son of one whose features, principles, and conduct I can trace in you. In the abyss of misfortune, he did not so much show courage as display all his honesty. The remembrance of spotless virtue fortified his last moments, as it had served to illustrate his whole life. Your destiny, given over to greatness, will not carry you away if you do not permit it to corrupt you. In the midst of honours and opulence, remember Fontainebleau, where you were poor, an orphan, and forsaken; and when you do recall these sad days, let them aid you to extend a helping hand to the unfortunate. I learn with great satisfaction that your young wife shares your sentiments; it is a proof that she also shares your love; and as I am interested in all that concerns her as well as you, it is in my *rôle* of mother that I rejoice with you. In this same *rôle* I embrace both of you."

I have thus presented to my reader this brilliant couple destined to give to the world a rare example of all the family virtues on a throne. We are now about to follow them step by step in their too short Court career, drawing attention in advance to the mutual proofs of tenderness and boundless devotion which these two lavished on each other until the day death came to divide them.

CHAPTER II.

Mutual Affection of Husband and Wife. — Their Popularity in Italy. — Eugene as a Patron of Arts and Sciences. — Napoleon advises him to amuse himself more. — Admirable Results of his Administration. — Satisfaction of the Emperor. He Names Eugene Heir Presumptive to the Crown of Italy.

I.

WE have seen how the Princess Augusta, betrothed at first for State reasons, learned to esteem and finally to love her husband devotedly. As to Eugene, his young wife soon inspired him with a deep affection, not only by her beauty, but also by her admirable qualities. In the midst of her Court, surrounded by the French and Italian ladies who composed it, she attracted all eyes by the brilliancy of her charms and the dignity of her carriage. Eugene hastened to assure Napoleon of the perfect happiness he had found in this union: —

"I am happy, Sire, in the companionship of the beloved spouse your paternal tenderness has bestowed upon me: she is sweet, amiable, and good; she is moreover grateful for the benefits received from you ; and her happiness will be complete if she continues to be worthy of your favours."

A contemporary, in a position to see what passed in the inner life of the husband and wife, says, —

" The Viceroy and Queen had never met before their marriage, but they soon loved as though they had known each other for years.   No two people were ever better mated.   There has never been a Princess, or in truth any mother, who has more tenderly cared for her children. She was born to serve as a model for all women.   An incident in this charming woman's life was told me which I cannot resist citing here.   One of her daughters, while still a child, had replied in a very rude manner to a lady's maid.   Her Serene Highness, the Vice-Queen, was told of the circumstance, and, to give her daughter a lesson, she forbade any of the household to perform any service for the young Princess or to comply with her demands.   The child was not long in coming to her mother to complain of this treatment.   The latter in a grave manner told her that, when she was so depending upon the services and cares of every one around her, she must learn to merit and recognise them by kindness and politeness.   She made her promise to apologise to the maid and to speak kindly in the future, assuring her that she would thus obtain any reasonable and just demand.   Her daughter obeyed, and the lesson profited her so well that she afterwards became, if the voice of public opinion can be believed, one of the most accomplished Princesses of Europe. The fame of her perfections extended even to the new world. She is to-day, I think, Her Majesty, the Empress of Brazil."

Augusta herself loved to assure Napoleon of the great affection she bore the husband whom he had given her, and she often wrote letters in this strain to the Emperor. A reply of his (1807) is here quoted : —

MY DAUGHTER, — Your letter has been received, and I note with the greatest pleasure the sentiments which you express towards the Prince. It has been a cause of much joy to me to learn that you are perfectly happy. I know that you have suffered much, and that you have shown courage under your trials.

Your very affectionate father.

The conjugal happiness of which the Princess writes, and in which Napoleon rejoices in his turn, was not destined to be of many years' duration. But at least it was cloudless, and would have been untroubled but for the formidable events of this period unique in history.

II.

The extract from Darnay's book which I have quoted elsewhere shows how triumphal was the young couple's journey across Italy, and how enthusiastically the people received their future sovereigns.

The radiant beauty, youth, and freshness, and the exquisite and adorable kindness of the young Princess captured all hearts. As to Eugene, he had already proved his merit. The people experienced his devotion in the zeal with which he knew how to defend the interests of his adopted country, and his energy in favouring all that could contribute to Italy's prosperity. He had thus become very popular. This did not deter him from giving new proofs of his capacity and watchfulness, as well as of his devotion to the Emperor.

He had hardly reached Milan before he gave himself up so arduously to his work that Napoleon — who, by the way, was not afraid of too much work for himself or others — thought it necessary to put a check on the ambitious young man by this affectionate reprimand: —

MY SON, — You work too hard; your life is too monot-
onous. This is not good for you; your work should be a
relaxation for you; but you have a young wife, and I
think you should arrange to pass the evening with her,
and gather some society around you. Why do you not
go to the theatre once a week, and make use of the
Royal Box? I think you should also have a hunting-
lodge, so that you could hunt at least once a week; I
would willingly add a sufficient sum to your budget for
this purpose. You must have more gaiety in your
household; it is necessary for your wife's happiness
and for your own health. If properly managed, a great
deal of work can be done in a short time. I lead the
life you do; but I have an old wife, who does not need
me to amuse her, and I also have more business to
attend to. And yet I must say that I take more pleasure and dissipation out of life than you do. A young
wife must be amused. You liked pleasure well enough
formerly. You must return to your former tastes; and
what you will not do for your own sake, you must do
for that of the Princess.

These last two days I have spent with Marshal
Bessières; we have played together like boys of fifteen.
You used to rise early in the morning; you must take
that habit up again. This will not disturb the Princess.
If you retire at eleven and finish your work at six in the
evening, you have ten hours for working by rising at
seven or eight.

Eugene evidently paid but little attention to
Napoleon's advice not to overwork himself. The

Emperor returns to the subject again, and this time points out grave reasons for obeying his commands on the working question, as it no longer concerns himself alone: —

MY SON, — I wrote you a short time ago, advising a hunting-lodge.   It is very important that the Italian nobility should accustom themselves to riding horseback; the exercise and the fatigue can only be for their advantage.   It is a great deal better for them to take this pastime than to be dallying around the ladies all the time.   Besides, this relaxation is absolutely necessary for you.

It is a rare thing for a father-in-law to write to a daughter-in-law, especially if the latter is young, beautiful, and captivating, reproaching her for leading too exemplary a life.   This was Napoleon's case, however.   He wrote to the Vice-Queen, during the summer following her marriage, and when Eugene was obliged to be absent frequently, —

MY DAUGHTER, — I can conceive the solitude which must be yours, all alone in Lombardy; but Eugene will soon return, and you never know how much you love a person until you meet the loved one again after an absence, — as we never appreciate our good health until we have lost it.

It is necessary in many ways that you should have company and amuse yourself.

All the news which comes to me from Italy tells me that you lead too quiet a life. I am always happy to obtain news of you, and I inquire of every one returning from your Court. It is very pleasing to me to learn that every one considers you perfect.

Even during the rapid campaign in Russia, which terminated in the famous victory of Jena, Napoleon found time to address a few loving notes to the Vice-Queen, such as this, dated from Berlin : —

MY DAUGHTER, — I received your letter. You do wrong to think that I could forget you. You know how much I love and esteem you. In all circumstances which may present themselves, you will have proofs which can leave no doubt in your mind.

Believe in my constant desire to do everything that is pleasing to you.

In another note he returns to his pressing admonitions that she should lead a gayer life:

MY DAUGHTER, — I received your letter. I read it with the same pleasure which I take in everything which comes from you. Try to be gayer and take more recreation than you do now. It is necessary at your age.

Eugene continued, in the mean time, to give himself up to his absorbing occupations with an indefatigable assiduity, as this extract from Baron Darnay shows : —

"Nothing which appertained to the Minister of War, to the direct orders of the Emperor, to his correspondence, ever left his cabinet; simple extracts from these letters were sent to the Chancellor, which touched upon business matters concerning him. The Prince worked not less than ten or twelve hours a day."

Each day a special courier set out from Paris for Milan, and in less than ninety hours bore the Emperor's despatches to Eugene, and with equal celerity carried those of the Viceroy to Napoleon. It was necessary to re-organise everything in this new kingdom, — the army, administration, tribunals, customs, and departments of all kinds. The impulse given by the Viceroy was so powerful that in six months after his arrival Milan was so totally changed as to be unrecognisable. Activity reigned on all sides, industries were making rapid strides, and the pomp and luxury so dear to Italian hearts were the order of the day. Although Napoleon scolded, he was well content, and he never ceased to give expression to his satisfaction with the Viceroy and his affection for him. He conferred the Order of the Iron Crown upon him some little time after his marriage. In reply to Eugene's letter of recognition for this favour, he wrote: —

My Son, — I am delighted to know that the decoration of the Order of the Iron Crown, which I sent you, has pleased you. I am happy circumstances are such that I can give you these proofs of my love. I can add nothing to the feelings I bear for you; my heart knows nothing dearer than you. These sentiments are unchangeable.

Every time I see you show evidence of talent, or hear something to your credit, my heart is filled with satisfaction.

Eugene, who always exhibited in the administration of his new kingdom a wise and enlightened moderation and an extreme watchfulness over his subordinates and subjects, at the same time gave ample proof of an energetic dignity worthy of the great man whom he represented.

When his enemies endeavoured to effect the landing of Anglo-Russian troops on the shores of Italy, Eugene defeated these plans by a series of measures so prompt and firm that Napoleon, upon learning of them, cried out anew, as he had already done on the battle-field of Austerlitz: " I well knew into whose hands I had confided my sword in Italy ! "

III.

It was at this time, during this marvellous epoch, that Napoleon seemed to fly from one victory to another.

This is the proud bulletin he sent to Eugene, after the battle of Jena, in which the Prussians were overwhelmingly defeated: —

MY SON, — The army of the King of Prussia no longer exists. The entire army at Jena (160,000 men) have been killed, wounded, or taken prisoners. Not one man crossed the Oder. I am master of their strong-holds, Spandau and Stettin; my troops are on the borders of Poland. The King of Prussia is across the Vistula. Barely 10,000 men remain to him. I am pretty well satisfied with the people of Berlin. I send you the different decrees which you need. The four regiments of cuirassiers should have set out ere this. Let me know when they reach the Danube.

And so this letter, written at the beginning of the new year, expressed his unceasing desire to see the Vice-Queen give an heir to France who would become a Prince and a soldier in the future: —

MY DAUGHTER, — For love of you, I have given orders that the members of the House of Strelitz shall

be treated with the greatest consideration. Your grand-
mother is very quiet. Your aunt, the Queen of Prussia, on the other hand, was very unruly; but she is so
unhappy to-day that it is unjust to speak against her.
I hope to hear from you soon that you have a fine boy;
but, if you give me a daughter, I pray that she may be
as amiable and as good as you are.

Napoleon's apprehensions were well founded.
A daughter was born on March 14, 1807, and
received, among others, the names of Maximili-
enne Eugenie. The Viceroy sent one of his
equerries to Paris, to announce the birth of her
grand-daughter to Josephine.

Notwithstanding his absorbing anxieties in his
operations against Prussia and Russia, Napoleon
found time to inquire for the health of the Princess. As soon as the news of the child's birth
was made known to him, he indicated by letter
to Eugene his desire that the baby should
receive a name dear to them both. Surely no
order could have been easier to execute: —

MY SON, — I congratulate you on the Princess's *accouchement*. I am impatient to learn that she is well
and out of danger, and I hope that your daughter will
be as good and amiable as her mother. It is a duty
with you to endeavour to have a son next year. The
means you have taken to record the child's birth are

very satisfactory. The Master of Seals must be instructed to send the papers to Paris, to be recorded in my family register. Have them addressed to M. Cambacérès, to whom I have made my wishes known. Have the little girl called Josephine.

The Princess Augusta was too near Napoleon's heart, too intimately one of his chosen family, not to tender him a filial affection in his sorrows as well as his joys. Thus at the time of the death of the Queen of Holland's young son, upon whose frail head Napoleon had for one moment thought of placing his own heavy crown, the Vice-Queen wrote a deeply affecting letter to Napoleon. The Emperor replied from the spot which marked the summit of his greatness, — Tilsit : —

MY DAUGHTER, — I received your letter of June 2d. I thank you for your kind words relative to little Napoleon. His mother is very unreasonable and mourns too deeply; we must have courage, and learn to resign ourselves to the inevitable. I am very anxious to see little Josephine, and hope that she resembles her mother.

Eugene bitterly regretted not having been able to take any part in the victories of Austerlitz and Jena. Urgent and exceptionally useful as was his rôle of Governor in Italy, he was disconsolate at being kept away from these battle-fields. But he was consoled at finding himself the father of a charming little daughter, and by the intense satisfaction which Napoleon showed when, towards the end of the year, he visited Milan to witness the excellent results of the Viceroy's incessant labours. The Emperor was so entirely content with the admirable organisation to which Eugene had brought his kingdom in so short a time, that he publicly announced, in default of a legitimate or natural heir, that Eugene should be his successor to the Crown of Italy. This was when conferring on him the title of the Prince of Venice.

The incoming of the New Year furnishing Eugene with an opportunity to thank Napoleon, the latter sent with the following despatch the gift dearest to the heart of a soldier : —

January 3, 1808.

My Son, — I thank you for your New Year's letter. I send you, as a New Year's gift, a sword which I carried on the battle-fields in Italy. I hope it will bring you good luck, and that you will use it with glory if the circumstances ever oblige you to draw it in defence of your country.

Eugene's work had been well worthy of Napoleon's approbation. When the Kingdom of Italy had been created, its army barely consisted of from twelve to fifteen thousand men. Now the government had by diligence brought the number up to fifty thousand men, well disciplined and ready to march upon the enemy.

Eugene had also effected miracles in his administration of the finances. Notwithstanding the great works of public utility and embellishment which he had undertaken, he economised for the benefit of the Italian treasury to the sum of ten or twelve millions a year, merely because he set himself the task of preventing fraud and wastefulness. His rigorous honesty earned for him, as we shall see later, the hatred and calumny of powerful enemies.

About the end of 1808, the Princess gave birth to a second daughter, who later became Princess de Hohenzollern. A few days later, December 31, 1808, Eugene, in renewing, as was his habit, his "absolute devotion" to Napoleon, could not restrain this cry of a soldier condemned to the inaction of peace when he burned with impatience to shine once more on the battle-field : —

" My life is entirely at the service of Your Majesty; and I find, to my great regret, that it is worth so little to you, since for so long a time it has been of so little use."

This noble consecration was soon to be accepted.

CHAPTER III.

The Campaign of 1809. — Mobilisation of the Army of Italy under the Command of Eugene. — His Private Correspondence with the Princess. — Italy Invaded. — A Defeat. — Bulletins of Victory. — Pursuing the Enemy. — March upon Bruck. — Campaign in Hungary. — Eugene wins the Dazzling Victory of Raab. — Triumphal Return to Milan.

I.

FOR some time Napoleon had been preparing the plans for a new campaign, and Eugene was called upon to take a most active part in it. Austria had fermented a national revolt among the fanatical inhabitants of the Tyrol. By inciting an uprising of the excitable students of the celebrated Union de la Vertue (Tugenbund), she had endeavoured to stir against Napoleon all Germany's young blood, at that time filled with a patriotic enthusiasm, and inspired with a horror of the French yoke.

Austria pretended to act in this war, not in defence of her rights, but as the liberator of Europe.

When war was declared, the Viceroy, for the first time acting as commander-in-chief, sent forth from Udine, where he had taken command of his troops, an energetic proclamation to his army. I will merely cull this extract as an example of military eloquence: —

"Generals, officers, and soldiers, you hold the title of the Army of Italy. Is there need for me to say more to you? Does not this title demand of you a repetition of the great deeds which it recalls? For a long time you have been suffering from inactivity; but thanks to your enemies, the day of glory has now dawned for you."

This proclamation is dated the 10th of April; but Eugene had already quitted Milan on the 4th of the same month to take command of the army. The day after his departure, at seven o'clock in the evening, he wrote to the Vice-Queen the first of a long series of private correspondence, filled with most tender and touching sentiments.

The reading of these letters, in which is depicted so delicately the soul of so lovable a man as was our hero, Eugene, caused me a tender emotion, which I hope will be shared by my readers. It is, so to speak, a romance of love, enclosed in the midst of the most startling

changes of fortune known to history, which I will
endeavour to place before your eyes.

Here is the first letter. You can perceive with
what ardour the Prince at once set about performing his duties. Arduous though they were, they
did not prevent him from frequently repeating his
sentiments toward his loved ones: —

VERONA, April 5, 1809.

I arrived at the gates of Verona two hours after noon,
my dear, good Augusta, and I at once mounted my
horse to pass the troops in review; afterwards I visited
the arsenal, and had hardly returned here before I
received a delegation of the city authorities. I am
about to sit down to table; it is seven o'clock in the
evening. After dinner I shall take a carriage and set
out for Trente and Lavis. I cannot tell if to-morrow
will be sufficient to enable me to inspect this part of the
country. We are having it very cold here. Last night
I did not close an eye. Would you believe it, we found
snow at Brescia, and that to-day, during my review, we
stood in it up to our ankles? There are three inches
on the ground everywhere; it is really extraordinary.
I hope your health is good, my dear Augusta, as that
of our little flock. I have scarcely left you all, and yet I
am anxious to see you again.

Adieu, my darling Augusta, my loving wife; you
know, I hope, my sentiments towards you; they will
never change.

The next day Eugene set out for the Tyrol. He wished to satisfy himself of the reality of these insurgent preparations, to reconnoitre the ground over which they would operate, and, above all, to find a good road for his artillery. The second letter, written two days after the first one, gives a detailed account to the Princess of this fatiguing expedition, partly made on foot: —

VERONA, April 7, 1809.

MY DEAR AND GOOD AUGUSTA, — I am just returned from my long journey into the Tyrol. Since I wrote you from here, — that is, the day before yesterday, — I have travelled two hundred and fifty miles, in carriage, on horseback, or on foot. There was a great deal of snow in the mountains. It was not possible for me to keep my *incognito.* I dined at the inn, with the principal men of the county; three of them were Bavarians. We, as you can easily understand, spoke of you; and, as you can also understand, it was the one subject which afforded me the most pleasure. Interested in the conversation, I forgot the hour, and midnight sounded as we were rising from table. I set out to-night for Mestre; and I can only stop over two hours at Vicence to inspect the troops.

I have little time to myself, as I am making out a full report for His Majesty on my journey through the Tyrol. I must draw this letter to a close, but not before expressing all my sentiments towards you. I beg you take care of yourself and of our two little cherubs, and I embrace all three as I love you, with all my strength.

Reaching Mestre at four o'clock, it was not until midnight, when his companions in arms were sleeping, and overcome with fatigue, that he could spare a few moments to send news of himself to his dear absent ones; and he wrote in the following terms: —

MESTRE, April 8, 1809, Midnight.

I can only write you a few lines, my dear Augusta. I passed a division of the army in review this morning at Vicence. I reached here at four o'clock, and immediately mounted my horse to visit the fortifications. On returning, I dined, and I have worked unceasingly until just this moment. All my staff are dozing and snoring on chairs in the neighbouring salon, waiting for me to get into my carriage. I will be at Udine to-morrow evening; there, as everywhere, you will always be with me, and my heart and my time are really divided between my work and the pleasure of occupying my thoughts with my little family.

I embrace you with all my heart, and our little love-pledges as well.

The same day on which he sent out his noble proclamation of which I cited an extract further back, proud of the fine condition of his men, his heart filled with a manly joy and confidence in

the future, Eugene wrote with adoring and loving
expressions, and in a delicately charming manner,
sending his kisses to the dear ones who were his
whole happiness.   He thus terminates a letter
dated from Udine (April 10th) : —

"Adieu, my good and tender wife. I finish with
regret, but not without renewing to you the assurance
of all my love. A thousand kisses to share between you
and our little ones. You will tell me how you distributed
them."

Certain severe critics may perhaps find this
way of expressing his affections as a husband and
a father too *bourgeois*.   But I hope that the
greater number may, like myself, find these letters
most sincere and touching.   They are the true
expression of a pure and strong love ; and that
alone is sufficient to ennoble them and to endow
them with real interest.

II.

The next day, April 9, 1809, hostilities being
commenced, the Prince hastened to re-assure the
Princess in these affectionate terms, and to calm
the loving uneasiness which he foresaw would be
hers : —

UDINE, April 9, 1809.

Rest perfectly tranquil, my dear and well beloved Augusta. War has been declared since yesterday morning, and, at a moment when least expected, our outposts were attacked; I am gathering my troops together. Do not allow yourself to be worried; I hope we shall come out of the affair in good shape. In spirit I embrace you.

The first engagement between Eugene's army and the Austrians was a victory for the Italians. From the battle-field, the young Viceroy sent these few rapidly written lines, which were worthy of being signed by Bernais: —

April 12, 1809.

You have doubtless been very uneasy during the last thirty-six hours, my very, very dear Augusta; and yet there was no reason for it. The enemy attacked us on all sides in pretty large numbers. The Austrians have lost five or six hundred men, and we have taken two hundred prisoners.

Good-by, my dear one; take good care of yourself and my little ones, and do not be frightened about me. A thousand kisses.

The first pitched battle, fought April 16, at Sacile, was, frankly speaking, lost. Eugene's generals, marching under his orders for the first time, felt little of the confidence so necessary towards the commander-in-chief, in this young man of twenty-seven years, and in consequence failed to co-operate as they should have done with him. The Austrians, it is true, had a much better organised and larger army than that put at his step-son's disposal by Napoleon. This oversight on his part was due to the fact that he had no thought of the enemy attacking the Italian army before the month of May. Indeed, this was the Prince's *début* as a commander, and he had his own personal experience to acquire. But all these excuses, notwithstanding their legitimacy, did not present themselves to Eugene. For him this defeat, after twelve years of military services commenced at the early age of fifteen years, was, to his mind, a humiliating one, and he cried out in anguish that never was there a battle so completely lost.

He was soon to make up for this disaster by a series of brilliant victories. The letter written to the Princess two days after his defeat is unfortunately lost, but in the following, it can be seen that while frankly acknowledging his reverse, he was no longer overwhelmed with despair as to the future of the French army, and that, in his unhappiness, he gave more thought to his wife's fate than to his own:—

TREVISE, April 18, 1809, Midday.

When I wrote you yesterday, my dear Augusta, I was in despair, because I had before my eyes the recent complete overthrow of our army. To-day I am more tranquil, and I have regained my courage; the enemy has not profited by his advantages, but I have profited by his idiocy, and have rallied my troops together. If the news from the Tyrol is good, there is still a great deal of hope for us. Adieu, my dear Augusta; rest tranquil. If, contrary to all expectations, the enemy marches from the Tyrol upon Verona or Brescia, you must at once take steps to leave Milan and go to Turin, even as far as Lyons, if necessary; this is in case of anything extraordinary happening. Adieu, my beloved Augusta. I tremble for your health; I am afraid this news will make you ill, and I am anxiously awaiting a reply to this.

The day after the battle, Eugene had not delayed confessing his defeat to the Emperor, without offering the slightest shadow of an excuse. "As it became," he wrote, "more necessary every day to open out on the enemy, I fought them yesterday, and I have the misfortune to be obliged to announce to Your Majesty that I lost the battle."

Then, after relating the circumstances, he added, anxious to take all blame from his subordinates, —

" It may appear extraordinary, but it is nevertheless true that several brave deeds were performed yesterday, and that our corps did their duty nobly."

Augusta, true to her charming character, wrote to her husband, three days after the battle, to try and console him for his defeat. We can see by the following how Eugene in his misfortune was deeply affected by this proof of affection, which, unfortunately, we are unable to reproduce here:

MESTRE, April 20, 1809.

Your letter of the 19th brought tears to my eyes, my dear, tender-hearted Augusta; no doubt I did wrong to give way to my disappointment, but when I wrote you, even a ray of hope was denied me. It seems that Chasteler is marching on the Tyrol; he has already passed Trente, and thus I am obliged to return to Adige. The army will be there two days.

The courage you have displayed calms my troubled spirit, and you well merit the loving sentiments I feel towards you.

With a charming feminine delicacy, to recall to him that even after having lost a battle he has not lost everything, the Princess sends him her portrait. Eugene thanks her in these few words:

TREVISE, April 19, 1809.

I have only time to write you a few lines, my dear Augusta. We have been very quiet all day; our spirits are reviving, and we already see a remedy ahead of us for all our ills.

I send a thousand kisses to yourself and our two little ones, and I am for life your loving and faithful husband.

I thank you for your portrait, which Lacroix transmitted to me this morning; nothing could give me greater happiness than to have my charming little family under my eyes.

But only one thing will bring back joy to the soldier's heart, and that is a victory. His only dream is to be able soon to measure his forces with the enemy, in order to efface the remembrance of his defeat. He writes from Vicence three days later: —

VICENCE, April 23, 1809.

I did not write to you yesterday, as I was on my horse nearly all day, and was very tired in the evening (you cannot imagine what trouble I have had in re-organising the army). The news from the Tyrol is very much less grave than I was led to believe at first. Adieu, my darling wife. I am well, but I shall never be perfectly happy until I have taken up the offensive (which will be in a few days, I hope), and more than all, when I can send you tidings of a grand victory.

Later, in the course of his march on the enemy, he writes: —

CALDIERO, April 26, 1809.

I embrace you in spirit, my dear and loving Augusta. I have been on horseback all day; I am impatiently awaiting the evening's reports of the enemy's position. I do not think anything new will turn up to-morrow. I am very well, and I am naturally desirous of doing something worthy of you.

Thus we see that he gives expression to his inmost thoughts to the Princess. He ardently desires success, that she should be proud of him. But the enemy evaded the encounter which Eugene sought so assiduously. The Viceroy openly took the defensive, and in his forward march gained a small victory, which argued well for the future. The fact that he could prove his readiness to enter the lists again with the enemy gave him great satisfaction : —

MONTEBELLO, May 2, 1809, 1 A. M.

From daybreak we have been pursuing the enemy, dear Augusta, and we have a slight skirmish at this place with his rear-guard. Our advance-guard, commanded by General de Broc, had a sharp encounter, and our troops only withdrew upon my orders ; we took about five hundred prisoners, and lost about forty men on our side. I hope to join forces with the enemy at Piave. I have received word from the Emperor, and he was not very angry at my lost battle. I am very well, and we are all very happy at the prospects of continuously advancing. I hope to find some faces ahead of us that will be much surprised at seeing us again.

Adieu, my darling Augusta; I love you and embrace
you, and through you our little cherubs.

Eugene redoubled his efforts to lose no chance
of meeting the enemy. He was on horseback all
day, and rarely found leisure to converse by letter
with his dear wife. This simple note of May 4th
speaks for itself : —

SAN–PIETRO, May 4, 1809.

Bonjour, my dear Augusta; I could not write you yesterday, and I have little time to do so to-day. I was on
horseback all day yesterday surveying the Brenta. The
Austrians have burned all the bridges, and I have been
obliged to construct rafts. To-morrow morning the
entire army will have passed over; their rear-guard
have been before us all day, but I think they will march
away to-night. But for a little fatigue, I am well, and I
love thee!

At last a bright day dawned for Eugene; it
would have been more brilliant still if the enemy
had not baffled him : —

CASTELFRANCO, May 6, 1809, 6 A. M.

Yesterday was a lucky day for us, my dear Augusta;
the results are: three hundred men killed, eleven hundred prisoners; our loss amounts to about one hundred
and twenty men. Yesterday I was at the head of all
the cavalry; as soon as we had crossed the Brenta, we
pursued the enemy for seven miles, with havoc for him,
but we were never able to bring him face to face with

us; I hope we shall meet him to-day on the Piave. Cavaletti can tell you all the details; but what he cannot tell you, are my loving sentiments towards you.

The pursuit continued unabated; but Eugene despaired of overtaking the enemy, and regretted the hours lost in endeavouring to force him into battle. At last, on May 8th, the occasion presented itself, and the Prince seized it with impetuosity. By a bold attack he succeeded in routing the Austrians.

The joy with which Eugene announced a real victory to the Princess, in a bulletin as laconic and precise as the success he had just gained had been rapid and complete, may easily be imagined: —

CORNEGLIANO, May 9, 1809.

At last I have gained a great victory, my good and tender Augusta. The Emperor will, I hope, be satisfied with us. Yesterday we made a very bold attack, for the army crossed the Piave in full view of the Austrian troops who were in retreat; and yet three fourths of my soldiers did not fire a gunshot. The cavalry covered themselves with glory. The results of the battle are: fourteen pieces of cannon, at least twenty-five to thirty caissons, three thousand prisoners, including two generals, eight staff officers, and forty to fifty other officers; besides which, they lost two generals, and three were seriously wounded. Give this good news out in Milan, and I hope the people will be pleased to hear it.

Adieu, my dear wife, I am going to try and follow up my success.

From that time on, success seemed to reward his every effort. Three days later Eugene defeated the Austrians at Saint-Daniel, and he sent a short note to the Princess announcing the fact: —

SAINT-DANIEL, May 12, 1809.

We fought a very brilliant battle yesterday at this place, my dear Augusta. The enemy's whole rear-guard were in position on the heights above this city; the firing had already commenced when I arrived with my advance-guard. I planned the attack, which was lively and successful: we made fifteen hundred prisoners, of which twenty-two were officers, and captured the flag of the Kieske regiment. The enemy lost more than six hundred men, killed and wounded; our loss might be estimated as being at two hundred and fifty men. The other divisions of the army arrived after all was over. I embrace you in spirit.

Eugene followed the enemy to the frontiers of the kingdom, — the Austrians trying to evade the risks of a great battle; and, in the letter which follows, the Viceroy jestingly scolds them for constantly fleeing: —

PONTEBELLO, May 15, 1809, Midday.

Here I am at Pontebello, my very dear Augusta, that is to say, on the frontiers of the kingdom; our outposts

are in Malborghetto, which the enemy had fortified: I
have been there this morning already, inspecting their
works.   These rascally Austrians, to enable them to
retreat more easily, have cut down all the bridges, and
there are two of them so completely ruined that it will
take at least a month to put them in condition for the
waggons to pass over.   You can judge how all these
inconveniences enrage me!   My health is very good;
I am very much fatigued, but I shall be well recompensed for all that if the Emperor is only contented.
Adieu, my dear Augusta; always continue to love me.
I embrace you, and through you our little ones; a kind
remembrance to the ladies of your Court.

III.

The campaign commenced to map itself out in
the most favourable aspect.   Driven out of Italy,
the Austrians began to prepare to defend their
own territory; but they were not long in retreating in great disorder before the attacks of the
Viceroy's army.   And in effect, on the 17th of
May, they were routed from their intrenchments
by a *coup de main*, redounding entirely to Eugene's
glory; for he, notwithstanding his generals' advice
to the contrary, ordered an attack on an enemy
protected by redoubtable strongholds, and gained
a complete victory, worthy of effacing in Napo-

leon's mind the remembrance of his preceding
defeat. Indifferent to the fatigue of such a day,
he was still up at midnight and writing these
lines to the Princess, breathing the joy of triumph,
and at the same time a warm affection coming
from the depths of his heart: —

May 17, 1809, Midnight.

I hasten, my dear Augusta, to announce my great
news to you. The 17th of May is for the Italian army
one of the most brilliant days in its military annals:
this morning we captured a fort looked upon as impreg-
nable, and yet our grenadiers took it at the point of the
bayonet. Nearly all the garrison were put to the sword;
they only took three hundred prisoners from us. I set
out at once to rejoin the advance-guard; I found them
at Tarvis. I immediately reconnoitred the enemy, and
made up my mind they were preparing to attack us last
night or this morning. Although there still remained
but two hours before daybreak, I mapped out the attack,
and it was made on my right, on which side was stationed the Italian division commanded by Fontanelli.
The fire was sharp, decisive, and successful; the rest of
the army had hardly time to fire a shot. The enemy
was chased for six miles in the greatest disorder. I
cannot just now compute the total result of the day, but
we must certainly have captured two thousand or three
thousand prisoners, twenty to twenty-five pieces of
cannon, and God knows how many we will gather up
to-morrow. The battle was a hot one; we have lost

about three hundred men, and the enemy's bullets tes-
tify in the ravaging evidences of their work of destruction to the fierce encounter of this great day.

I hope the Emperor will be content; I myself am well
satisfied.   I tell you this in confidence: I am more than
content with myself, from the fact that this attack was
my own idea, and that I was advised against it, on
account of the enemy's strong intrenchments; but I held
to my given orders, and the result has proved my good
judgment,— a few hours later, and we should have been
defeated ourselves.   I am very well.   For the last few
nights I have not slept at all, but everything is going
along smoothly.   Adieu, my dear Augusta; announce
this good news to your Court, and love me as I love you!

The decisive success of the Grand Army, under
Napoleon, and Eugene's unrelenting pursuit were
a severe reverse to Archduke John, General of
the Austrian troops. Four days after the date
of the preceding letter, Eugene was at Klagenfurth, in Carinthia, *en route* to join forces with
Napoleon's army. As can be seen by the few
lines addressed from this place to the Vice-Queen,
if he found time neither to sleep nor to change
his clothes, he still found plenty of time to think
of his cherished companion: —

KLAGENFURTH, May 26, 1809, 6 P. M.

Here I am, encamped at Klagenfurth with a part of
the army, my dear Augusta; and four leagues farther on,

at Marburg, is my light infantry. We shall probably march seven or eight days longer without meeting the enemy, as he is retreating in great haste; and in the mean time I am manœuvring to join the Emperor. I could not write yesterday, as I had worked a great deal and slept but little; but I told Bataille to write to Madame Wurmbs. I receive your sweet letters every day, and I hope you realise all the pleasure they give me. It has rained here excessively all day. I have no change of clothes with me, as my baggage is two days' journey behind me, and I am afraid I cannot get it before to-morrow; I am like a little Saint John, with a single coat on my back, for I have lost my cape. Those bridges destroyed by the enemy have played the devil with us.

Five days later Eugene gained another victory, at Saint-Michel, when he attacked and routed the most important corps in the Austrian army. The animated picture of this happy day, which he drew for the Princess, is not overdrawn, if we compare it with the accounts of contemporaneous historians. For instance, Seel writes, —

" About two o'clock, the attack commenced along the line. Before the fire had fully developed, Eugene arrived with the rapidity of lightning to take command of the troops. He at once ordered the assault at bayonet-point; the heights of Saint-Michel were soon the scene of terror and disorder among the enemy's troops, who fled in wild dismay."

But let Eugene speak for himself : —

SAINT–MICHEL, May 26, 1809, 6 A. M.

Again good news, my darling Augusta; but this news is really excellent. I was fortunate enough, after three days of extraordinary marching, to be able to overtake the corps of the Austrian army commanded by General Jellachich, who was defeated by the Bavarians at Salzburg, though since then he has had some success. This corps, reinforced by several battalions, came from the interior and took up their position in front of us yesterday morning, after a march of forty miles, upon the slope of Saint-Michel (it is a superb position). I reached the outposts at eleven o'clock. I at once arranged the plan of attack. I hurried a second division to my assistance; and this corps of Jellachich's, seven or eight thousand men strong, was totally annihilated in two hours: hardly six hundred men gained the mountains. General Jellachich saved himself with only sixty dragoons ; the Austrians had eight hundred killed at least, twelve hundred wounded, and we have already counted forty-five hundred prisoners, of whom seventy are officers. You will read more details in the papers, and you will no doubt see the names of Triaire and De Lacroix mentioned; they made some splendid charges.

I am very well satisfied, because I think the Emperor will be. It is a great thing for us to have destroyed a corps of the Grand Army. They assure me that General John is at Gratz; if he comes to Bruck, we shall meet him to-night or to-morrow. There are barely

twelve or fifteen thousand men left of this brilliant
army of fifty thousand. It was of the utmost importance to prevent the reunion of Jellachich and Prince
John. In one month we have captured twenty thousand prisoners and one hundred and forty pieces of
cannon from the enemy.

I beg of you, give these good tidings to my sister and
mother, as well as to the King of Bavaria; I have not
time to write to them. Tell them also to your Court.
I like to think that they will please the people of Milan.
Adieu, my dear Augusta; you know my love and tenderness for you, and that they will never change.

Eugene reached Bruck in Austria with an
unheard-of rapidity, and the 27th of May he effected his reunion with the Grand Army. The
Emperor was delighted with this bold step, and
cried out, on learning of it, "Nobody but
Eugene could have reached Bruck to-day; the
heart alone is capable of accomplishing such
marvels!"

The Emperor addressed a proclamation to the
Italian army, in which the well-merited praises
were very flattering to Eugene and his soldiers.
He hastened to impart them the next day to
the Vice-Queen: —

BRUCK, May 28, 1809, 12.30 P.M.

I am overwhelmed with joy, my dear Augusta; the
Emperor wrote me a charming letter, as soon as he

learned of our junction. He appears well satisfied, and he has ordered me to publish in the Italian army the enclosed proclamation. You will see by it that he gives proof of his great satisfaction with my actions. Really we have made unheard-of marches, notwithstanding the battles and the numberless obstacles the enemy has placed in our path. I hope all these good tidings will please Milan. The King of Bavaria will also learn with joy that we have destroyed the corps of the army which worked him the most injury.

At last Eugene arrived in Vienna, May 29th, and at once set out to find the Emperor at his headquarters at Ebersdorf, a quarter of a mile by carriage from the city. He reached there about five o'clock in the evening. Baron Darnay, who had the honour of accompanying him, and was the happy witness of the flattering reception the Prince received from His Majesty and the whole staff, relates how the Emperor hurried to meet Eugene in the doorway and pressed him closely in his arms, then presenting him to the marshals and the Major-General, cried out: " It is not only courage which brings Eugene here, it is his heart also ! "

The same evening of this cordial reception, the witness goes on to say: " The Emperor seemed to be carried away in an extraordinary manner by his admiration of Eugene." The latter, with his accustomed modesty, contented himself with writing these few lines to the Princess: —

EBERSDORF, May 29, 1809, Midnight.

I reached here at midday from Vienna, my dear Augusta, and I immediately repaired to the Emperor's headquarters. He was extremely kind and loving to me, and repeated that he was well satisfied with me and my manœuvres of the Italian army.

IV.

The campaign, however, was by no means ended. The enemy tried to concentrate and reorganise their forces in Hungary, where Arch-Duke John had retired with the remains of the Austrian army, together with the Crown jewels. Napoleon ordered Eugene to attack and shatter this last hope of the Hapsburg monarchy. The young Viceroy felt that now was his opportunity to revenge his first reverses, and threw himself with ardour upon the work before him.

On June 9, he wrote from Sarvar in Hungary:

SARVAR, June 9, 1809.

You know that I left the Emperor five days ago, and that I have come in search of the Archduke John at the head of my army. We were all most anxious to

meet him again before he crosses the Danube.   The
Emperor has treated me so kindly that I am more
than anxious to please him, and will do all that I can
to accomplish his desires.

Adieu, my dear Augusta, rest quietly; we are all
well, notwithstanding our long marches.

I have now come to what was perhaps the
most brilliant day in Eugene's life, — that of the
14th of June, 1809.   That day the Viceroy gained
the famous battle of Raab, which cost him more
than six thousand men.   This battle was fought on
the anniversaries of Marengo and Friedland ; and
Napoleon, famous for uttering words which were
afterwards destined to become historical, bap-
tised the battle of Raab as " The grandson of
Marengo ! "

When one has been on horseback twenty hours
out of the twenty-four, and, like Eugene, does not
even give to sleep the time strictly necessary,
there is little time in which to write as constantly
and fully as one desires.   Thus it happened that
it was not until the next day the Viceroy took
up his pen to write the following succinct letter :

SZOMBATHELY, NEAR RAAB, June 15, 1809.

I send Tascher, my dear, good Augusta, to bring news
of me and reassure you.   It is several days now since I
have been able to write to you, for I have been on

horseback twenty hours at a stretch. I won three
battles this month, the 11th, 12th, and 13th; and yesterday, the 14th, the anniversary of Marengo and Friedland, I won a brilliant victory over the army under
Prince John.

The combat was the fiercest I ever saw in my life.
To oust the enemy from his position, we were repulsed
six times. At the seventh attempt we succeeded in
reaching the summit of the plateau. Our losses, while
not amounting to those of the enemy, were yet considerable. Authouard, Triaire, and De Lacroix, on our
side, were wounded. Delbreme received a bullet-wound
in the abdomen. Several of my officers and pickets
were killed, and Petrus (Mameluke), who was behind
me, was wounded in the head. All these details are
now in the past, and I can give them to you. We have
captured two flags, and the Hungarian insurrection will
water its wine after this adventure. I think we must
have had yesterday in front of us nearly twice as many
as our own men. Tascher will give you all the details.
The Emperor has named him as my aide as well as
Jules de Serres, who was aide to the Minister of War,
and the young Labédoyère, who was aide to Lannes,
and of whom great things are said. Adieu, my good
Augusta; I am a little tired, for in the last eight days
I have actually not slept six hours.

To Napoleon, Eugene announced his victory
in these simple words preceding the exact rela-
tion of the facts: —

SIRE, — I hasten to acquaint Your Majesty with the fact of a battle fought yesterday with Prince John, and that I was lucky enough to win it. It was the anniversary of too grand a day to allow us to suffer misfortune.

This letter is dated the 14th, the day of the battle. On the 16th, Napoleon replied from Schoenbrunn : —

" I congratulate you on the battle of Raab. It is the grandson of Marengo and Friedland. Announce my satisfaction to the army."

Napoleon's praises were honestly deserved. It was remarked that during this campaign Prince Eugene took more prisoners and captured more artillery than he himself had men and cannons under him.

In the midst of the fatigues of war and the manly joys of victory, Eugene's heart never forgot the more intimate pleasures of the far-distant fireside.

It was from Raab that he addressed the following letter, more like that of a lover than a husband : —

IN THE CAMP AT RAAB, June 22, 1809.

MY VERY DEAR AUGUSTA, — I have calculated that this letter will reach you on the day of your anniversary, and that it may be more certain, I send it by my courier, Tortes; I cannot send it by an officer, as all mine are on sick beds. I offer you on the 21st what I offer you every day, the expression of my deep love. It is frank, passionate, and lasting, much more so than any words can express. I have been away two months and a half. A long time, is it not? But have I not been well recompensed by the way in which the Emperor has treated me, and fortune has smiled on me? Confess that I was born to be happy, and you know how large a share you hold in my happiness. The battle of Raab was grand. The enemy lost one thousand men.

The bombardment of Raab was directed by Eugene with a pitiless energy. It lasted for two days; and during this time this man, so sensitive to generous sentiments, suffered from the rigours imposed upon him by war. His heart was riven in hearing, amid the thundering of the cannon, the cries from the half-consumed city. He turned his eyes from this heart-rending spectacle, endeavouring to forget it in the loving contemplation of beings so tenderly cherished. In touching terms he traced for the Princess the following picture of those awful days : —

IN THE CAMP AT RAAB, June 23, 6 A. M.

Instead of reopening my letter, my good Augusta, I write you a second to announce the capitulation of

Raab. We have bombarded it pitilessly for two days, and about half the city is burned. It was heart-rending to listen to the cries of the unhappy inhabitants all during last night. We were going to make a breach to-day, and to-morrow perhaps order an assault. They did well to surrender.

I do not think, though, that the capture of Raab will mean a rest for us. We are prepared to march at any moment; and a happy thing for us is that we are always ready and well disposed to march.

Adieu, my dear Augusta; I send a thousand kisses for you and my little angels. I gazed on your portraits this morning. My heart filled with pleasure, but this happiness is as nothing compared to that which will fill me when I press you in my arms once more. Adieu.

The city was finally taken. He entered in triumph among the smoking ruins, which, as he wrote his wife the following day, "were but piles of rubbish."

In the mean time, the Emperor was concentrating his forces at Vienna in view of a decisive battle, which was to rank among the greatest battles of the century, that of Wagram. Eugene received orders to retrograde the Italian army from Raab in the direction of Vienna, where he was to work in conjunction with the Grand Army. The Prince and his men contributed largely to the success of these two bloody and triumphant days. They took twenty-five hundred prisoners from the enemy and captured eight pieces of cannon. The next day, July 7, the Emperor, crossing the bivouacs of the Italian army at eight o'clock in the morning, stopped before the tents and said to the soldiers, "You are brave fellows; you have covered yourselves with glory."

This victory won Napoleon the peace of Vienna and cost the Austrians eighty-five millions and their beautiful Illyrian provinces. The next day Eugene thus announces the exploits of his army to the Princess : —

IN CAMP BEFORE STAMERSDORF, July 7, 1809, Morning.

Victory is ours. My dear Augusta, I am well, except for a little fatigue. We fought for forty-eight consecutive hours. The Italian army covered itself with glory. The Queen's regiment of dragoons deserve special notice.

Eugene was delegated by Napoleon to protect Vienna against any aggressive return of the Austrians. His troops were to be placed *en échelon* in such a manner that his command extended over a very important part of the Empire. During this whole occupation, the excellent discipline which he maintained over his men, the humanity with which he treated the inhabitants, endeavouring thus to soften the rigours of war, excited the esteem and recognition of all.

On the 12th of July, still in ignorance of the armistice signed that very day, he wrote the Princess this charming letter, in which his regret at being so far from all his loved ones is so delicately expressed : —

SIEBENBRUMER, July 12, 1809.

Now that the great battle is ended, you should be very tranquil. It is true the affair lasted two consecutive days and was very hotly contested, but it is impossible that there should be two such battles in one campaign. I was happy in the midst of the cannon's roar, as I always am; but I should have thought my felicity exhausted had I had you and my dear little ones with me. Would you believe that on the day of that battle there were one hundred and fifty thousand cannons fired, and that thirty thousand of them were aimed at my corps of the army?

It will be a happy moment for me when I can take you and my little ones in my arms once more.

Following Napoleon's example, Eugene, in the midst of his labours as Commander-in-Chief of the army, did not neglect the cares of his government. He profited by the leisure which the armistice afforded him to devote himself assiduously to the affairs of his kingdom.

He hardly permitted himself from time to time

the relaxation of hunting. But neither the responsibilities of a general, nor the preoccupations of a viceroy, nor the pleasures of the hunt, for one moment obliterated the image of the adorable wife who was his idol. What touching simplicity there was in this " *bonjour*," at the reveille of the soldiers!

PRESBURG, July 18, 1809, 6 A. M.

Bonjour, my dear Augusta. My first thought this morning, as every morning, is for thee and my pretty little ones. I received your letter of the 7th yesterday. It came by way of Strasbourg. I knew that the Emperor intended to announce the armistice by equerry to you. I did not know of it until thirty-six hours later, and during this time I fought on the march as if those last cannon-shots were meant for me.

V.

From that moment peace was looked upon as being very near at hand. It was, however, the 14th of October before it was signed, and the winter had come before Eugene found himself free to return to his family, who missed him so much. His isolation weighed more and more heavily upon him, and upon the 19th of July he wrote to the Princess:

PRESBURG, July 19, 1809.

I leave here to-morrow morning, my very dear Augusta; and as I shall be two or three days on the road, I hasten to notify you. I am going to visit the battle-field of Austerlitz, and I shall profit by this little journey to reconnoitre the country.

Yesterday evening, Tuesday, I was thinking of our little games, and I regretted them very much. It seems I shall be very well placed at Eisenstadt. They tell me there is a superb park there filled with game. I intend to hunt every morning, work afterwards, and think of my little family all day.

Oftentimes the roads were infested with the enemy's spies; and, as the couriers could not pass, it frequently happened that the Prince was without news from home for days. He suffered from this deprivation greatly, as the following letter shows, — a letter in which Eugene gives free rein to his sentiments as faithful husband and loving father: —

VIENNA, July 22, 1809.

MY DEAR AUGUSTA, — I have just returned, and I hasten to impart my news to you, and it is very good. I came here to spend three or four days with the Emperor. I leave here for my headquarters in Hungary. I saw Louis (Prince Royal of Bavaria) this morning. He has gained greatly since I last saw him. We breakfasted together with the Emperor, and I hope we shall see a great deal of each other during the few days we remain here. You can imagine of whom we spoke. You were the constant subject of our conversation, as you are always of my thoughts.

The news of Eugenie's two teeth has pleased me greatly, and everything points to her getting the rest without any trouble.

Allemange joined me at Brunn, and remitted me all the mail delayed at Udine. I have your fourteen letters! All that I suffered in waiting for them is amply made up by the pleasure in hearing such good news of my little family. Adieu, my dear, good Augusta; I hope we shall not be separated much longer. I embrace you and my two little ones, and I love you with all my heart. Your faithful husband and friend.

For her birthday, Eugene sent the Princess a present from Vienna — "a bagatelle," as he calls it — with these lines, in which he depicts the tender intimacy, the happiness, and the exquisite simplicity of this princely household: —

VIENNA, July 26, 1809.

I send Bataille with this letter, my dear, good Augusta. It is near your birthday, and I hope this will reach you just at the desired moment. I send you a bagatelle from Vienna, which I thought very pretty, and I hope it may seem as pretty to you. I will not offer you any new protestations of tenderness and affection for the 3d of August. These sentiments are the same and will be for all days and time. I send you some playthings for my little angels; and I hope that Josephine will pay you her little compliment, and I only regret that I am not there to teach her a prettier one. I hope that the news of the armistice will quiet Italy; I was pained to learn of those petty revolts. We are getting in readiness to reopen the war, but everything leads us to believe that matters will straighten themselves out. I know not when I shall see you and press you in my arms; but you know, I hope, that this moment, when it does arrive, will be one of the happiest of my life.

Now that the excitement of battle no longer occupied all his thoughts and tired his body, Eugene lived in Milan more than in Vienna. He entered into the smallest details of the Princess's existence, worrying over a slight illness which she had concealed from him, and talking to her in terms which were much more those of an ardent lover than of a husband. Here is a pretty billet which he wrote her, to explain his great regret at not being with her on her fête-day:

VIENNA, August 3, 1809.

To-day is the 3d of August and your fête-day, my dear Augusta; and it is with regret that I remember I am not near you to give expression to my sentiments. How happy all those who are near you at this moment must be! I slept at Schoenbrunn last night, as it was late when the play was over; and this morning Prince de Neuchâtel and myself hunted together. We returned for parade and breakfast with the Emperor. Aubert has just told me that your foot hurts you still; why did you not tell me about it? Adieu, my dear Augusta; I love to think that in the midst of the pleasures of your fête-day you will still think a little of my regret.

On her part, the Princess felt this protracted separation keenly; and notwithstanding all her courage and her desire not to cause the slightest worry to her husband, she could not hide the sadness which filled her heart at the prospect of a still longer duration of the campaign. Eugene, upon receipt of a letter in which he read between the lines the sorrow she so bravely tried to conceal from him, hastened to reassure and comfort her: —

" Clerici has just brought me your letter. Its contents dashed my cup of joy from my lips, my dear Augusta. In it I could read your sad thoughts, and I swear to you, you should not have them. Believe in me; in our star, which is a happy one; on my conscience, which will always be pure; on the justice of the Emperor, and the bonds of love which unite us."

And he scolded her gently for not confiding her smallest worries as wife and princess to him. Did not their hearts, closely united, form but a single soul, in all that was common between them, — sorrows, joys, hopes, and the anguish of love? Here is a letter which plainly outlines his idea of what should constitute an ideal marriage: —

VIENNA, August 26, 1809.

Why is it that when you are sad you hide it from me, and keep it to yourself? You know me but little, my dear Augusta, and you give me little credit for my sentiments towards you, if you keep silent on your troubles. You can confide them to no one who will sympathise with you more than I, and I must confess you have hurt me. If I were to know that you were worried, if I were to see you with sadness in your eyes, I could only say to you that you were wrong. Yes, my dear Augusta, you wound me deeply when I know that you are worried and anxious over a future which can be nothing but a happy one, for the omens since our union have been most favourable. But what would hurt me more than anything would be to know that I was shut out from your confidence. Put these sad thoughts and ideas away from you, because they are not worthy of you, and there is no reason you should have other than agreeable ones; if you feel sorrowful sometimes, it is on your husband's heart you should lean for comfort, — he who has no other interest than yours; he who is devotedly and entirely interested in you. Adieu, my dear friend; do not look upon this as a scolding, I pray you. I have opened my heart to you, so that you shall always read therein my tender and unchangeable love for you.

The Princess sent Eugene, upon his twenty-eighth birthday, a present which could not be otherwise than agreeable to him, — her picture and that of his children. The joy which he felt, burst forth in this sweet, simple, and delicately lover-like epistle : —

EISENSTADT, September 4, 1809.

I thank you a thousand times, my darling Augusta; I saw Anoni yesterday. I returned here yesterday evening at eight o'clock, very tired with the heat of the day and the hours spent in travelling, never giving my twenty-eight years a thought. I had hardly reached my room before Anoni was announced. Judge of my happiness when he handed me your letter and your charming gift. The idea was a delightful one; the portraits very like, especially that of Josephine; indeed, they are all admirable. I will carry them with me everywhere; they will recall to me, every time I gaze upon them, the happiness which is mine in my little family. I am going out almost immediately, as the Emperor has ordered me to hold several reviews. I will send Anoni to Vienna, which city I shall reach late this evening, and I will keep him with me several days, so that I can talk about you more at my ease.

Bonjour, my dear friend; I have not the time now to explain to you how much touched I was by your kind attention, and how happy you have made me. Adieu, my beloved Augusta; you well merit and possess all the love of your faithful husband and friend.

Desirous as he was for the peace which would enable him to return to his loved ones, Eugene was none the less sensible of a new proof of Napoleon's confidence. His tenderness as a husband was not overshadowed by his ardour as a soldier : —

VIENNA, September 12, 1809.

Anoni has told you no doubt, my dear Augusta, that
we talked long and often about you, and that my
thoughts are filled with the happiness of once more
feeling your arms about me; this happiness will, I hope,
be possible next month, for I have strong hopes that
everything will be ended here by November 1. (This is
for you alone.) I set out day after to-morrow for Holla-
brunn, where the Emperor has ordered me to hold
cavalry reviews; and I shall be absent two days. The
Emperor has added four regiments of light cavalry to
my corps, making in all three thousand horses; this
division is a grand one, and I shall have more than nine
thousand cavalry under me. Adieu, my good and
tender friend; our preparations for war are on a grand
scale, and yet you can in all certainty count on a near
peace.

The "Adieu" which ended each of Eugene's
letters to the Vice-Queen was always charming,
and breathed a sentiment of profound delicacy.
In one, in which he announced that the Emperor
was about to visit the troops, and "hoped the
Emperor would be pleased with their condition,"
he terminated by saying: "Adieu, my dear Augusta; I embrace you as I love you, that is, tenderly." The day after, September 20th, giving a
description of an enjoyable day he had spent
hunting, he finished thus: "I have a pile of

letters to read, so far I have only opened two; you do not need to be told whose. Adieu."

I have a letter before me, without historical value, but which appears characteristic because of the intimate and familiar tone in which the Prince acquaints the Vice-Queen with the smallest details of his daily existence, — details noted hourly, so to speak, and which are so precious to two hearts united by a strong tie, for this knowledge enables them to live each other's lives while separated : —

Vienna, September 23, 1809.

I could not write to you yesterday, my dear Augusta, as I had intended to, for we were on horseback nearly all day. The Emperor was drilling his Guard, and placed me in command of his cavalry. For several hours we were, so to speak, in mimic war. In the evening I was somewhat fatigued, but it is all gone now. I have nothing new to tell you. The weather is getting quite chilly; and I hope sincerely we shall not remain here long enough to see snow in Vienna.

I received a letter from the Empress day before yesterday. She told me she had written to you the day before; her health seems good, and my sister writes me from Plombières that the waters are doing her good. I saw the young Prince of Darmstadt on parade this morning. I gave him your compliments; he begged me to send his in return. I think I told you that on the

Emperor's fête-day he had a fall from his horse, which laid him up for over two weeks. He was obliged to keep his bed, but is fortunately on the high-road to recovery. Adieu, my dear Augusta; think of the pleasure of meeting again. That will console you for absence, especially when you remember that the pleasure cannot be much longer delayed.

Ah! as to that so ardently desired return, he thought of it ceaselessly, and it can easily be imagined with what joy he welcomed the slightest indication of its near approach. " They talk," he wrote September 24, " of the near approaching journey of the Emperor to Paris, and consequently of my turning my steps homeward. That day will surely be one of the happiest in my life."

The nearer he felt that day approaching, the more Eugene forgot the victorious hero of Raab, and became the loving husband and the affectionate father. From Vienna he sends some playthings to his " petites choux," accompanied by these simple words : —

" I hasten to send you good news, my dear Augusta. Three Austrian generals arrived in Vienna yesterday from Schoenbrunn, to consummate the treaty. It is certain now that everything will be quickly arranged. I now repeat what I have already told you, that I shall see you before the month of October is over. If the weather is not too bad, remain at Monza. I should like to spend a few days there. I send you by the courier, to-day, some toys for the little ones; kiss them both from Papa, and receive the assurance of my loving tenderness."

Eugene comforted himself with the hope of his approaching return; he could only think of his beloved ones, and he consecrated every spare moment which the duties of his high position left him, to making all kinds of purchases in Vienna. Who can read the passionately loving words which terminate the following letter without being affected?

VIENNA, October 1, 1809.

Nothing new for the last two days, my dear Augusta. The Emperor is still in conference with the Austrian generals, and I hope all will soon be settled satisfactorily.

I still cling to the hope that I shall be with you on Saint Hubert's day. I have bought you some beautiful pearls, toys for the little ones, and I still hope to purchase a good piano for you.

To occupy myself with you is the relaxation of my days, as to love you is the happiness of my whole life.

In the following lines the same passionate desire to clasp his adorable wife in his arms once more, and the loving thoughts which fill his mind, are delightfully depicted: —

VIENNA, October 6, 1809.

Everything is progressing fairly well: detachments of the Guard had set out, *en route* to Munich; but the Austrian plenipotentiaries showed a cloven foot, and they were recalled. However, this evening the news has gone around that peace will be signed in two days. In forty-eight hours I can tell you positively, and perhaps think of my own departure. I do not speak of how much I think of you, for you are not out of my thoughts one instant. I have been making numerous purchases the past few days, — horses, pianos, engravings, porcelains; these last are for you, and I hope they will please you.

VI.

The good news which was to bring such happiness to Eugene and his sweet wife was at last announced. Peace was signed, and he hastened to acquaint the Princess on the 14th of October. But, alas! nothing in this world keeps pace with the yearnings of love. Eugene was constrained to have still more patience, for Napoleon had need of him. He was obliged to remain with the army until the ratifications were exchanged, to review the troops, to pacify the Tyrol, to organise the States wrested from Austria, before the sun rose on the ardently desired, long-looked-for day of reunion : —

VIENNA, October 15, 1809.

Yesterday peace was signed, my dear Augusta; this should free you from all worry, and I hope your health will be better in consequence. All you have to think about now is the happiness of meeting. This happiness, if retarded for the moment, cannot, however, be delayed much longer. I received new instructions from the Emperor this morning. He leaves to-morrow, but he has ordered me to remain in Vienna until after the ratifications, and to review the several divisions; thus, you see, I shall be detained several days. Afterwards the Tyrol must be pacified, the newly conquered States organised; and His Majesty has charged me with all this. But I can assure you I will get through as quickly as I can. I hope to be at Klagenfurth on the 25th of the month, where I shall be obliged to remain for several days. I will keep you informed of my movements every day. I am filled with joy in thinking that I am drawing nearer and nearer to you daily. I have written to the Minister of Public Worship to have a *Te Deum* sung throughout Italy. It would be well for you to have one sung in your private chapel. If the weather becomes too bad, and you can no longer remain in the country, I think you had better return to Milan. It is very damp and chilly here already. You cannot imagine how busy I am and will be. Nearly all my men move as soon as the ratifications arrive.

On his arrival at Klagenfurth, that pretty little capital of Carinthia, — one of the most pictu-resque spots in Austria, — a new and grave obstacle faced him, and threatened to delay the moment of his well-earned repose. Far from quieting down, the insurrection started in the Tyrol by Austria's perfidy seemed to take a new life. Was Eugene to be detained in quelling a revolt, instead of joining his loved ones?

KLAGENFURTH, Morning of the 27th of October, 1809.

Here I am at Klagenfurth, my dear Augusta. I shall remain here until to-morrow, because the troops I am to take into the Tyrol will not reach here until then. When the people know that peace has been signed, I hope they will listen to reason, and we shall not need to use force. In any case, the result is certain. The Emperor has placed three divisions of my army at my disposal, — the division stationed at Trente, and the three Bavarian divisions which are at Schlesburg, and which have already commenced moving towards Innspruck. I like to think that I shall not need to make use of all my forces. I am not more than two days distant from you, my beloved one, and my fondest hope is soon to be still nearer to you. Adieu.

The Princess, as impatient at this enforced separation as Eugene, proposed to join him if he was to be further prevented from joining her. Uncertain of the turn affairs might take, he had the courage to refuse this loving offer, or at least to delay its execution : —

" Our letters will take only two days in reaching us.
I am only two days and a half journey from you, and
I hope soon to be able to join you, if only for a few
days. It is better for you to wait for me. If I find I
cannot go to Milan, I will endeavour to arrange some
way by which you can come to me."

Unhappily the insurgent Tyrolese, carried away
by the voice of their chief, Andreas Hofer, the
intrepid innkeeper of whom I shall speak later,
showed no intention of laying down their arms.
The prospect, when so short a distance separated
him from Milan, caused Eugene great grief : —

VILLACH, November 2, 1809.

I received very good news from the Tyrol this evening, my dear Augusta. General Baraguay d'Hilliers announces that he hopes to enter Linz without firing a
gun. I have hastened to inform the Emperor of this
fact, in order to hurry my return to Milan. You cannot imagine how distasteful and tiresome this country is
to me. I worked all day yesterday; I passed half an
hour last evening with my staff; and they, poor fellows,
had great difficulty in concealing their yawns. I played
a game of chess with Triaire, and retired at eleven
o'clock, in very bad humour with the cold, the bad
weather, my present occupation, and my enforced absence from you.

After an interval of three days, he writes, —

VILLACH, November 5, 1809.

To-day is the feast of Saint Hubert, my very dear Augusta. Just a year ago, we spent such a delightful morning together at the Villa Augusta. Here, we are not only not hunting game to-day, but we are at a loss how to chase away the ennui which is tormenting us. I say us, for I can see the gentlemen of my staff yawning from morning until night; and if it were not for the ten or twelve hours of work, I should be doing likewise.

I have not yet received my courier from Linz this morning. If the Tyrolese quiet down, I hope to get away from here before long. I am anxious to embrace you and my two little ones, but in waiting for this happiness I send all three a million kisses.

That same day Eugene wrote the Princess a long letter on the subject of the reproaches made to him by his father-in-law, the King of Bavaria, apropos of his proclamation to the Tyrolese.

To comprehend the difference which had arisen between the King of Bavaria and Eugene, I must say a few words as to the origin and progress of the Tyrolese insurrection. The Tyrol had belonged to Austria until Napoleon had forced the vanquished Emperor to cede it to his ambitious ally, the King of Bavaria, at the Treaty of Presburg, shortly after the electorate had been raised to the dignity of a kingdom. Austria, secretly hoping to reconquer the Tyrol, had, by means of agents, fermented a national revolt. Vanquished anew, she had abandoned the poor Tyrolese to their fate. Eugene, whose natural kindness of heart always leaned towards humanity and clemency, first tried means of conciliation. He issued a proclamation to the people of the Tyrol, in which, though demanding their submission, he promised the insurgents " to hear their grievances and listen to their requests."

" Tyrolese," he said, with great nobility, " if your grievances are well founded, I promise you that justice shall be done you ! "

This proclamation, strictly conforming to Napoleon's views, grated on the exaggerated susceptibilities of the King of Bavaria. The Princess Augusta's father looked upon the Tyrolese as rebellious subjects, unworthy of clemency, and needing extreme measures to recall them to their duty.

My Beloved Son, — You should remember that in acquiescing to these demands to listen to the grievances of the Tyrolese, you degrade my sovereignty. This is not the proper language to use to rebellious subjects; it encourages them to rebel again at the first opportunity.

This was not Eugene's view of it, and he explains his actions thus to the Princess: —

VILLACH, November 5, 1809.

I was greatly grieved this evening, my dear and good Augusta; and as I hide nothing from you, I hasten to acquaint you with its cause. You have perhaps read my proclamation to the Tyrolese. I venture to say it was good, for I have already seen its effects. As my troops advance, the inhabitants retire to their firesides. You know me well enough to be certain that I put nothing into that proclamation but what I was told to say. Certain phrases displeased the King, and he wrote me this letter, a copy of which I enclose you. I am very much hurt, and I replied to him this morning. I also enclose you a copy of my letter, and deliver myself to your judgment. Do not speak of this to any one, — it is not necessary; but I must confess I was very angry that the King did so little justice to my character.

He has been sadly misinformed when he has been told that this country could be reclaimed by force. Kindness was absolutely necessary; and I do not think that the dignity of a sovereign would be offended in listening to the grievances of a people, — above all, as these people have returned in an orderly manner and laid down their arms. I curse this mission a thousand times. There is neither honour nor glory in its successful issue; and there is nothing but disgrace for me, if matters turn out badly.

Adieu, my dear, good Augusta; you and my little

ones are my only consolation in this world. It is a century since I wrote to the Empress and my sister, but I have not conscientiously had the time. Give them the latest news of me, I pray you.

The Viceroy's reply to the King of Bavaria was worthy of both of them. He wrote as a son-in-law should write to the father of a wife to whom he owed all his happiness, but at the same time as a man and a Viceroy, who knew his real duties to the throne. Notwithstanding the length of this letter, it throws so vivid a light upon the nobility of Eugene's character that I think it my duty to present it almost as it was written:

"Your Majesty seems to complain of the sense of my proclamation. I have the honour of informing you that I was simply executing the Emperor's orders. I feel it my duty at the same time to state that I should have taken it upon myself to announce to these rebellious people that I would listen to their grievances and see that justice was done them. It could not enter into my mind to be oblivious to the dignity of a throne to which I am bound by ties of sentiment and whose glory will always be as dear to me as my own. But I thought that the most essential thing in an expedition such as this is, was to succeed and to prevent as much bloodshed as possible. Besides, my aim was to persuade them to grow calm and to lay down their arms. But in order to obtain this end, it was necessary to give them a ray of hope; and it was this ray of hope I held out to them when I said that we would listen to their grievances and render them justice. I bound myself to nothing positive in advance, and yet it must be in Your Majesty's heart to do justice to all your subjects.

"Who knows whether the real truth with regard to the Tyrolese has reached your throne? Perhaps some dishonest agent has treated these people as it was not in Your Majesty's heart they should be treated; sovereignty is not degraded by listening to your subjects' grievances! These people, it is true, were armed yesterday; but to-day they are disarmed, and ask pardon for their error, at the same time praying that justice be done them. This is the sense of my proclamation. I beg Your Majesty to pardon me, if I become warm over this matter; but I am anxious that you should understand the sentiments which animated me and the intentions which I entertained. Besides, I have seen enough of the country and its inhabitants to know that you will gain nothing from them by force. If we declare war, we shall only lose a number of brave men, and conquer in the end a country in ashes and unfortunate for centuries to come."

Two days after his last letter to the Princess, Eugene conceived anew some slight hopes of being at last reunited to those who were dearer to him than all the world. But, in any event, his movements depended on the exigencies of his command. With this man, everything — even to

the most legitimate aspirations of his heart —
yielded to duty.

VILLACH, November 7, 1809.

I have this evening received very good news from the
Tyrol. The disarming is taking place very tranquilly.
In some places on the mountains, our soldiers were received by gun-shots; but, following out my orders, they
did not return the fire. In several villages the peasants
have taken up arms for Bavaria. You see by this that
patience and a desire to succeed, will put down any
mutiny. I assure you, I should much prefer an active
campaign than to recommence a parallel duty. My
success gives me great pleasure, and I am only awaiting
news from His Majesty. I hope his orders will enable
me to rejoin you shortly. The 11th corps of the army,
by orders from the Emperor, is about to march forward
and occupy Frinne and Croatia. If this takes place
quietly, I am at liberty to repair to Milan; but if they
have the slightest trouble, I cannot in conscience leave
my army scattered over two hundred leagues of country; and I must, whether or no, remain where I am.
All this is supposititious on my part, and may never
happen.

Eugene's noble heart revolted at the idea of
scattering death among these ignorant mountaineers, poor abused peasants, excited by their priests
and by Austria's spies, and now hemmed in by
the reunited armies of Napoleon and the King of
Bavaria. Obliged by Napoleon's orders to send

a corps of twenty-six thousand men, taken from the Italian army, to co-operate in the Tyrol in conjunction with the Bavarian army, the hero of Raab and Wagram ceased not to call this campaign "a miserable war!" He had no other wish than to retire, if this could be done consistently with his duties as Commander-in-Chief.

His most earnest desire was to return to Milan in time for his fête-day, the 15th of November. What joy that would be for his beloved wife! But whether this return was possible or not, he desired that the Princess should be happy on that day.

VILLACH, November 11, 1809, 7 P. M.

I am very seriously thinking of setting out; and you may rely upon it that I shall exert every effort to arrive by the 15th, — it may be in the morning, it may not be until evening. I am awaiting tidings to-morrow which will decide the question. If it so happens that I cannot reach home on that day, I beg of you to be happy; and that will be easy, for I shall surely be very near you and ready on the instant to clasp you in my arms.

At last the ardently desired moment arrived. Eugene announced to the Princess that he would set out at once. It had been decided that the Italian corps of the army which was to go into the Tyrol should be commanded by General

Baraguay d'Hilliers, under the superior direction of the Viceroy, who would direct its operations from Milan.

The following are the joyful lines in which Eugene announces his departure: —

VILLACH, November 12, 1809, 5 P. M.

I am just about to get into my carriage, my dear Augusta, to fly to you; I send this letter ahead by the courier, who is in charge of my horses. I assure you that I shall follow him as fast as possible; you may rest assured of my intense desire to embrace you!

Before accompanying Eugene into Italy, I should add a few words as to the fate of these poor Tyrolese, so cruelly duped by Austria, and that of their audacious chief. After Eugene's proclamation which I cited above, Andreas Hofer decided to lay down arms and enter into negotiations with the Viceroy. He wrote him in the following terms : —

"It needs neither time nor trouble to rouse a people irritated by oppression; but it needs much of both to calm them. A feeble spark is sufficient to fire a city, and millions of hands can hardly subdue this incendiarism.

"Monseigneur, deign to hear the last prayer I dare address you: permit a deputation to wait on you, in order to recommend the people of the Tyrol to your clemency.

" It is buoyed by this consoling hope, that I place the expression of my submission at the feet of Your Imperial Highness ! "

In a second letter Hofer renews this submission in still more explicit terms : —

" Monseigneur, the Tyrolese people, confiding in the goodness, the wisdom, and the justice of Your Imperial Highness, place through us, their fate in your hands. They are ready to lay down their arms, if by this means they can obtain your good-will and protection. They have much to complain of; for Austria, by her recent perfidious insinuations, precipitated the insurrection ! "

Would any one believe that after this double submission Hofer would have again ignited the brand of revolt ? This was what he did, however. After a slight success at Saint Leonard, a new proclamation, fanatic and inciting, was spread broadcast over the Tyrol, calling the people under the banner of rebellion.

" God," Hofer says, " has chosen us for His own people, and has ordered us to do battle against a strange nation, the most powerful on earth. We will fight like the chevaliers of old, and God and the Blessed Virgin will give us their blessing ! "

Notwithstanding the desperate resistance of the insurgents, many of whom died at the point of the bayonet; notwithstanding the rocks which the enraged mountaineers rolled from great heights upon the French troops, — this bloody insurrection was promptly crushed on January 27, 1810, and Hofer was taken prisoner.

Eugene, who knew how to appreciate courage, was touched by the heroism which Hofer had always displayed during this terrible struggle. He had tried to save him. He might perhaps have succeeded, if the intrepid mountaineer had been willing to take back his last proclamation. But the latter preferred to die, a martyr to the cause, and, at the price of his life, pay a debt which Austria had so badly recompensed. Much against his own heart, Eugene was forced to execute Napoleon's laconic order, which was a death-sentence : —

MY SON, — I wrote to have you bring Hofer to Paris; but since he is at Mantua, order a military court-martial, have him tried and shot on the spot. Let this be a matter of twenty-four hours only!

Thus this terrible insurrection, which Eugene had thought to quell by kindness, ended bathed in blood. This pitiless repression made a hero, a martyr, of Hofer, whose memory the Tyrol venerates to-day !

CHAPTER IV.

Divorce. — Josephine's Resistance. — Eugene's Intervention. — His Admirable Disinterestedness. — The Empress at Malmaison. — Relations between Josephine and Napoleon after the Divorce. — Eugene and Hortense's Filial Devotion. — The Prince's return to Milan. — Grave Consequences of the Divorce for Eugene.

I.

THE cannon which announced the Viceroy's return to Milan was also the signal for great rejoicing. The loyalty and sweetness of his character had gained the affections of his subjects, as the charms of the Vice-Queen had attracted the most cordial homage of her Court. But the prominent part which Eugene had just taken in the last campaign against Austria had crowned him with a fascinating aureole whose splendour was reflected on the happy Princess and his government. Alas! while Eugene awaited in the sweet felicity of his renewed family happiness the *fêtes* which were in preparation all over the kingdom, to welcome him joyfully home, a thun-

derbolt was about to strike him, from the clear
and unclouded sky.

The Treaty at Vienna, in weakening Austria,
which deprived it of three millions and a half
inhabitants, had raised Napoleon, though already
master of the Continent, to the summit of his
power.

It was at this period that the regret of having
no direct heir grew in the conqueror's heart.
Josephine having had no children during the
fifteen years of their marriage, he had built
his hopes at first on the eldest son of Queen
Hortense ; but the child's death at the age of four
awakened him rudely from his dream. Napoleon
would gladly have adopted Eugene ; but a Beauharnais could not, as the Emperor declared, under
these painful circumstances, become the master
of the Bonapartes. Besides, Napoleon's brothers
(especially Joseph, who was the eldest of the family and was particularly jealous of his rights) would
certainly have raised innumerable obstacles in
his path.

On October 26, hardly fifteen days after the
Treaty of Vienna was signed, Napoleon gave the
first evidences to far-seeing eyes of the resolution
which he had formed. On returning to France,

instead of joining the Empress at Paris, where she awaited him, he stopped at Fontainebleau, where Cambacérès, the arch-chancellor, received orders to join him.   There was held a secret conference lasting several hours, in which Napoleon declared that he desired a direct heir to his throne and power; that his brothers were not fitted to reign, being profoundly jealous of each other, and in no way disposed to obey his successor if the direct heir were not such a one as the law would force them to recognise.   During all the negotiations he showed a marked preference for Eugene, praising his character, his services, his modesty, his boundless devotion, but declaring that no adoption would be sufficient to make him acceptable as the heir to the Empire after his death.

He was resolved to obtain a divorce.   Cambacérès protested in a timid manner at first, dwelling on Josephine's popularity and the fond remembrances which joined her past with that of Napoleon's at the dawn of his marvellous career.   He explained that the army, attached to the recollections of the Revolution, would view with displeasure a daughter of the House of Hapsburg or Romanoff taking the place of one

Napoleon.

who had wedded the brilliant Republican general and mounted step by step beside him in his grandeur. To all these objections, Napoleon, to cite Thiers's majestic language, " replied, as absolute master, whose will ruled the world, and had in a measure become destiny itself, ' He must have an heir; this heir obtained, the Empire, even after his death, was permanently founded.' "

Josephine, alarmed by this mysterious conduct, so contrary to Napoleon's usual habits, went to Fontainebleau in the afternoon. The Emperor, feeling himself insufficiently prepared to announce his irretrievable decision, hesitated to acquaint her with his determination. He, in fact, feared the effect of Josephine's anguish upon him, and desired to await Eugene's arrival, knowing that he alone was capable of softening the violent shock which the awful truth could not fail to produce.

Husband and wife returned to Paris; but Josephine, with that fine perspicacity of women, at once divined the blow that Napoleon intended to deal her, and burst into tears. Her daughter, Queen Hortense, was summoned. The two poor women at first attempted to soften Napoleon's heart, and turn him from the dreadful project which they foresaw. But what could their tears accomplish in opposition to this iron will? Napoleon was not the man, once his decision was made, to allow himself to be dissuaded from a plan, especially if his personal ambition was in question. Hortense was so overwhelmed by her mother's despair that she would almost have preferred the brutal avowal of the sad truth to the torments of a devouring uncertainty.

II.

So painful a situation could not be prolonged. Napoleon, to put an end to the anxiety of all, decided to summon Eugene, whom Josephine had already, in her great grief, called to her aid.

November 26, the Empress wrote to the Viceroy of Italy: —

My Son, — I desire, if no important business prevents you, that you set out from Milan so that you can reach Paris by the 5th or 6th of December. Come alone, with three carriages and four or five of your suite. Pass through Fontainebleau. This is supposing that nothing of vital importance prevents you from carrying out these orders."

What sad days preceded Eugene's arrival, in this royal family whose closest intimacy had been so rudely broken!

Every one could notice the great change in Josephine's features and the silent restraint of Napoleon. If, during the dinners of these lugubrious days, between the 26th and 30th of November, the Emperor broke the awful silence, it was only to ask brief questions, the answers to which he did not even listen to. The storm burst on Thursday the 30th. Their Majesties were seated at table ; Josephine wore a large white cap, partly hiding her face and knotted under her chin. She had been weeping, and seemed hardly able to restrain her tears in the presence of the domestics. Her face was a living picture of anguish and despair. A deep silence had reigned during the meal. They merely tasted of the viands placed before them for form's sake. The only words spoken were those addressed to the Comte de Bausset, —

" What kind of weather is it ? "

As Napoleon spoke thus, he rose from the table, Josephine slowly following his example. Coffee was brought in, Napoleon helping himself to a cup, which a page tendered him, and signifying by a gesture that he wished to be alone.

Every one retired; but soon were heard heart-rending cries from the Emperor's salon, and the voice was recognised as being that of Josephine. One of the gentlemen-in-waiting, thinking she was ill, rushed to the door, which was suddenly opened by Napoleon himself, and upon perceiving the Comte de Bausset, he said quickly, —

"Enter, Bausset, and close the door."

Bausset, entering the salon, perceived the Empress lying prone on the carpet, moaning and sobbing.

"No, I will never survive it," she cried.

"Are you strong enough to lift Josephine and carry her to her apartments by the private staircase?" Napoleon asked, turning to the Count. "Give the Empress into the care of her maids, and see that she receives all the attention her pitiful condition calls for."

Bausset obeyed, and lifted the Empress, who, he thought, was suffering from an attack of hysteria. He carried her in his arms with Napoleon's assistance. The latter, taking a candle from the table, lighted it and opened the door of the salon, which gave upon a dark passage-way leading to the private stairway. Warned at the first steps, Bausset observed to Napoleon that the staircase was too narrow to make it possible for him to descend without danger of falling.

The Emperor called the Keeper of the Portfolio, whose duty it was night and day to remain
stationed at the door of the cabinet, opening on
this private stairway. Napoleon handed him the
candle, of which there was no longer any necessity, as the passage-way was lighted, and then
ordered him to pass first and take the feet of
the Empress. She was then carried down, not
without great difficulty, and laid on a lounge in
her bedroom. The Emperor called her ladies-in-
waiting and passed out, followed by De Bausset,
into an adjoining salon, his agitation and ner-
vousness being extreme. In his trouble he informed the Count of all that had just happened.

"The interest of France and my dynasty,"
he declared, "does violence to my heart. This
divorce has become a stern duty for me — I have
been worried, anticipating the scene which has
just occurred — as I have been anticipating it for
three days, since I knew the Empress had been
told by Hortense of the unhappy obligation
which condemns me to separate from her — I
pity her from the bottom of my heart, but
I thought she was stronger-minded than that,
and I was not prepared for such a paroxysm of
sorrow."

His emotion forced him to long pauses between each phrase; his words escaped him in an incoherent, jerky manner; his voice trembled, and tears stood in his eyes. Indeed, he must have lost his usual self-possession to enter into details with a man so far removed from his counsel and confidence. This scene did not last more than seven or eight minutes.

Napoleon at once sent for Corvisart, Queen Hortense, Cambacérès, and Fouché, and before returning to his own apartments went to assure himself of the condition of Josephine, whom he found calmer and more resigned.

When Eugene received the orders to repair to Paris, he was in the most complete ignorance of Napoleon's plans. The Emperor, as I have already said, did not wish to take any official or definite steps before his step-son's arrival.

By a singular coincidence, the Viceroy, returning from Austria to Italy, made his entry into Milan the same day that Napoleon, with his divorce fully resolved upon, had announced his intentions to Cambacérès at Fontainebleau. The Municipal Council had unanimously voted, in honour of the Viceroy's victories, a grand ball at the Scala, and a public ball in the Porto-

Risconosenza Gardens. A solemn *Te Deum* was
to be sung in the cathedral the next day; and the
public ceremony of dowering sixty young girls, a
charming idea, emanating from the Prince, was to
close the *fêtes*.

But Eugene was not to enjoy the pleasure of
assisting at these rejoicings. His sky, so serene,
was suddenly overshadowed, and instead of thrill-
ing with joy at the sound of popular acclamations, he was destined to wipe away the scalding
tears of an anguished mother.

III.

The Vice-Queen, representing her husband
during these *fêtes*, was more joyful than uneasy,
for she imagined — and not without reason —
that perhaps the Emperor had called Eugene, the
hero of whom she was so proud, to him, to pro-
claim him heir presumptive to the imperial crown.
What bitter thoughts were hers when the first
letter informed her of the sad truth!

A new alliance on Napoleon's part cast sombre
shadows of uncertainty over the brilliant present
and the future filled with marvellous promise,
which was offered to her husband; an heir,

Napoleon's own flesh and blood, crushed all her hopes of the grand throne of France. Was it not to be feared even that the crown of Italy, which had dazzled her eyes before her marriage, might not vanish also like a deceptive dream?

To celebrate the glorious Peace of Vienna, Paris was given over to grand *fetes* on Napoleon's triumphant return. The grandeur of these *fêtes* was enhanced by the presence of many princes and allied sovereigns. The King and Queen of Bavaria, the King of Saxony, and the King of Württemberg had come to Paris to join the circle of princes of the Imperial family, of whom Their Majesties of Holland, Westphalia, and Naples formed a part. What irony in the contrast between these sumptuous rejoicings and the misery which filled Josephine's uneasy soul, devoured by jealousy and despair!

"I do not really know," writes Mademoiselle Avrillon in her Memoirs, "whether she was more unhappy in the blow which had been dealt her, or in the preliminaries of the event itself. Notwithstanding the conviction of her future, she still nursed, if not hopes, at least a vague uncertainty of thought; and each time a minister or grand dignitary of the Empire came to see her, she plied him with indirect questions, equally tormented by the desire to know her fate, and by the fear of learning it. But every one was dumb, and only evasive replies were given her."

For the sake of public opinion, which the Emperor was not ready just at present to enlighten, Their Majesties continued to live seemingly together; and certainly one would never have doubted they were still united by bonds of love, so courteous and attentive to every little want of the Empress did Napoleon show himself.

Waiting for Eugene, the Emperor had requested his sister Hortense to remain near Josephine. He hoped that the generous efforts of her two children would inspire the Empress with the courage to face the awful necessity of the approaching supreme crisis in a dignified manner. In this he was not mistaken.

The noble attitude of Queen Hortense during these awful days of waiting was a guarantee of her brother's conduct, when brought face to face with this cruel upheaval of their fortune and common future. She assured the Emperor that Josephine's children, satisfied at renouncing the grandeurs which had not made them happy, would voluntarily consecrate their lives to consoling the best and tenderest of mothers.

Such quiet dignity, such grandeur in her dis-interestedness, moved Napoleon deeply. His eyes were filled with tears. What a touching scene, to see the conqueror of the world weeping, because, from a fatal stroke of politics, which he was not strong enough to resist, he felt himself constrained to repudiate the spouse his heart had chosen, the companion of his earlier glory and his best days! He no longer commanded, he implored, Hortense to remain near him to assist Eugene in calming the agonies of the woman he still loved.

Josephine found herself the recipient of the most tender care from Napoleon, — attentions which overstepped their mark and were more sorrowful than beneficent for the victim, for until her son's arrival they encouraged her to keep up the hope that Napoleon would relent. Nothing definite, in fact, had been said ; the irreparable word would perhaps never pass Napoleon's lips.

Vain illusion, which Eugene's presence dis-pelled at once !

Eugene's arrival was preceded by a little inci-dent which will bear repeating, as it shows into what a condition of over-excitement and suspicion Napoleon had fallen, under the weight of the heavy secret which he desired to guard at any price until the hour fixed upon for its execution.

Josephine's cousin, Commandant Tascher (later General Count Tascher de la Pagerie), was attached to Eugene's suite as aide-de-camp. As he wished to return to France to visit his parents, the Viceroy, taking advantage of his work in the Tyrol, sent him to Paris to give the details on the suppression of the Tyrolese insurrection to Napoleon, and at the same time to see his cousin, the Empress.

On arriving in Paris, Tascher went straight to the Tuileries, and his presence was announced to the Emperor. What was his astonishment to be asked in Napoleon's most brusque manner, —

" Are you sent here by Eugene to spy upon my actions? "

The young Commandant had hardly time to stammer out a reply, when Napoleon, thinking he had already seen Josephine, demanded, " Have you seen your cousin ? "

" No, Sire ; I have just arrived, and my post-chaise is still in the courtyard."

This assurance finally dissipated the Emperor's suspicions. He questioned Tascher for a few moments, and opening a door leading to the Empress's apartments, dismissed him, saying, " Go down ; visit your cousin."

Tascher found Josephine in her little salon. She, upon seeing him, flung herself into his arms, sobbing and crying out, —

" He abandons me. He wants a divorce. Where is Eugene ? "

Tascher informed the Empress that her son suspected nothing; and it was agreed that the young aide-de-camp should go to Hortense at once, and beg her to go forward and meet Eugene in order to prepare him for the distressing news awaiting him on his arrival in Paris.

IV.

Eugene had left Milan on the 1st of December. On the 3d he wrote his wife a few lines from the hospital of Mont-Cenis. This traveller's billet, waiting a change of horses, offers in itself but a secondary interest, but it proves what I want to establish, and that is, that he was still in entire ignorance of the terrible blow awaiting him : —

" Here I am just arrived at the Hospital of Mont-Cenis, my very dear Augusta ; and as my carriages are somewhat behind me, I am going to eat a morsel and indulge in remembrances of you.   The mountain is very difficult just now.   It took the Queen of Naples three days to make the passage."

The Prince had the pleasure and the surprise, also, of embracing his sister before reaching Fontainebleau.   It was a doleful interview which was held between the Viceroy of Italy and the charming Queen of Holland, unhappy wife and mother, and the bearer of still greater news of unhappiness.

Eugene reached Paris in the morning of the 7th of December.   He at once wrote to his wife : —

PARIS, December 7, 1809.

I arrived this morning, my very dear Augusta.   My sister came as far as Fontainebleau to meet me, and as I would have reached Paris late at night, I preferred to sleep at the former place.   I was very happy meeting my dear sister once more.

I could not tell you the reasons for my journey, my beloved, before my departure, for I was in ignorance of them myself.

After a résumé of the news he had heard from Hortense, he continues, —

" It is indispensable for the Emperor's peace of mind that all this terminate favourably.   You know me well enough to understand the position in which I find myself.   What sustains me through this terrible ordeal is the knowledge that I possess your heart, and that your sentiment, like your soul, is above all happenings. I saw the King of Saxony at the Tuileries this evening.   We spoke of you most of the time.   I will make all my visits of etiquette to-morrow; I cannot tell when they will be over.

" Adieu, my dear friend; I love you and shall love you all my life, as well as our two children.   I shall be back in Milan much sooner than I anticipated."

His letter despatched, Eugene hastened to Napoleon, who received him with honest affection, pressing him to his heart as formerly, and assuring him that his tenderness for himself and his mother had never changed.   He then explained to him the State reasons which obliged him to separate from an unfruitful wife, and to sacrifice the hopes of the Prince himself, explaining that a Beauharnais could never reign over the Bonapartes.

On leaving Napoleon, Eugene, with a broken heart, but firm countenance, sought the Empress. The interview was most touching.   His mother's great grief seemed somewhat assuaged by the boundless love of her son.

He with his penetrating judgment needed but a glance to see that all these struggles were telling on his mother's health, and that it was for Josephine's best interests to arrive at a definite solution quickly. He begged Napoleon to grant the Empress a decisive interview which would put an end to these uncertainties, more cruel than the sad truth.

This interview took place on the same evening, and Josephine submitted to the sacrifice which the Emperor deemed necessary for the welfare of France ; but foreseeing the uncertain fate of her children, she addressed this supplication to Napoleon, broken by sobs and tears, —

" Once we are separated, my children will be forgotten. Make Eugene King of Italy. My mother-love will be satisfied; your policy will be applauded, I dare predict, by other nations."

" No," Eugene interrupted ; " I do not wish that there should be any question of me in this affair. Your son does not wish a crown which shall be the price of your separation."

And sadly he added, repeating on his part the disinterested words Hortense had uttered a few days previous, —

" Our mother must go away. We must go with her; and together we will expiate in retreat the ephemeral grandeur which has been a sorrow rather than a pleasure in our lives."

Napoleon, deeply moved by so much nobility, mingled his tears with those of Josephine and her children, whom he begged to remain near him.

Seeing his mother about to renew her supplication to the Emperor for his future, in accordance with his dignity as Viceroy, Eugene put an end to it by words worthy of the greatness of his soul: —

" If you submit to the Emperor's will, it is you alone of whom he must think."

And Napoleon cried out, —

" I recognise Eugene's heart.   Indeed, he is right to rely on my love for him."

Much has been written on this celebrated theme.   Numerous versions have been published, but the most interesting is that of Madame Rémusat: —

" Eugene had declared to Napoleon that he would accept nothing at a moment of such deep sorrow to his mother, and that he would follow her into her retreat, even to Martinique itself, sacrificing everything to the need she had of consolation at such a time.   Bonaparte seemed struck with this generous resolution, though he listened in surly silence."

Constant, who had overheard a part of the conversation between Eugene and Napoleon, gives
the following very curious version : —

"Several days after the festivities, the Viceroy of
Italy, Eugene de Beauharnais, arrived. He learned
from his mother's lips the terrible step which circumstances had rendered necessary. This confidence overwhelmed him. Troubled, in despair, he sought His
Majesty; and, as if he could not believe the news he
had just heard, he asked the Emperor if it were true
that the divorce must be. The Emperor replied by
an affirmative sign, and with sorrow depicted on his
countenance he extended his hand to his adopted
son.

" ' Sire, permit me to leave you.'

" ' What?'

" ' Yes, Sire; the son of one who is no longer Empress
can no longer remain Viceroy. I will follow my mother
into her retreat. I will console her.'

" ' You wish to leave me, Eugene, — you? Ah, do
you not know the many imperative reasons which force
me to take such a step? And if I obtain this son, — the
object of my dearest desires, this son so necessary, — who
will take my place to him when I am no longer here?
Who will stand in the place of a father to him when I
am dead? Who will bring him up? Who will make a
man of him?'

"The Emperor's eyes were filled with tears as he
uttered these words. He took Prince Eugene's hands

in his, and, drawing him to him, embraced him tenderly.   I could not hear the end of this very interesting
conversation."

No one was better able to describe to us the
inmost facts of Josephine's conduct during this
trying ordeal than Mademoiselle Avrillon, her
chief lady-in-waiting.   In speaking of the night
following the all-important interview, she thus
describes Josephine's condition when she entered
her room to awaken her in the morning : —

" As I approached the bed, I found her in a condition
that was absolutely pitiable : her eyes were red and
swollen, and were mute witnesses of the tears she had
shed during the night.   Then it was that she told me
all that had passed the night before; she said the
Emperor had declared that he had decided upon a
divorce, and every word she uttered was interrupted by
her sobs.   I could not restrain a cry of surprise, which,
happily, was not heard outside.   The sorrow which I
showed on learning this sad truth put me in a condition of despair which I did not understand myself,
for the Empress in turn tried to console me.

" She excused the Emperor, against whom, in the
first moment of my surprise, an expression of anger
had escaped me.   'He is disconsolate,' she said, 'at
the idea of separating from me; he has told me so
himself; he has given me proofs.   He wept as he said,
" It is one of the greatest sacrifices I have had to make

for France." He told me that,' repeated Her Majesty,
and with what a persuasive tone she spoke! ' Yes; I
know he must have an heir to his glory, a child, who
shall live after him and consolidate his Empire. I
cannot doubt his love for me. He has sworn that he
will never oblige me to leave France.'"

During 'these painful emotions and about the
time of the official ratification of the divorce
by the Senate, Eugene received from his wife
this beautiful letter, in which the heart of the
Vice-Queen reached the grandeur of that of her
husband : —

MILAN, December 13, 1809.

I do not know what I wrote you yesterday, my dear
and well-beloved husband: the news of the divorce
overwhelmed me; my sorrow is greater because I suffer
for you. I picture your sad position; and, though far
from you, I can see the joy and triumph depicted on
the countenances of our enemies. But they cannot
do you the injury they would, because they cannot take
away your spotless reputation and your conscience without reproach. You have not deserved these misfortunes.
I say "these," as I suppose they are preparing others
for us; I am prepared for anything.

I regret nothing if your love still remains to me;
on the contrary, I should be happy to prove to you that
I love you for yourself alone. I cannot write to your
poor mother; what should I say to her? Assure her of
my love and respect. You say your return is near.

These words assuaged my sadness, and I await you with
impatience. Do not for one moment believe that I will
let myself be beaten. No, my Eugene; my courage
equals yours, and I am anxious to prove to you that I
am worthy to be your wife. Adieu, dear husband;
continue to love me, and believe and trust in the love
which I consecrated to you till the hour of my death.

V.

M. de Méneval, private secretary to the Emperor, and a witness to the inner life of the
Tuileries during the weeks which preceded the
formal act of dissolution of the imperial marriage,
thus speaks of the relations between Napoleon
and Josephine and their condition of mind during
this critical period : —

"Painful as these fifteen days must have been to both,
they nevertheless appeared very short to Josephine,
who could not accustom herself to the idea of losing her
rank as reigning Empress, and, above all, to the separation from Napoleon, whom she loved devotedly.

"The Emperor softened these last moments of their
union by acts of affectionate attention. He occupied
himself with her future, gave her advice, and forestalled
all her desires. Josephine possessed an irresistible
attraction; she was not regularly beautiful, but she was
endowed with a grace much more attractive than beauty,
as our good La Fontaine puts it.

Pauline Bonaparte.

" She had the soft languor, the supple, elegant movements, and the negligence of the creoles. Her temper
was equable, sweet, kind, affable, and indulgent to every
one without excepting any person."

To arrange the legal forms and ceremonials
of the divorce, Napoleon held a second interview
with Cambacérès, in which the smallest details
were decided upon. The Emperor declared that
" Josephine's future should be magnificently assured. She should have a palace in Paris, a
princely residence in the country, an income of
three million francs, and the first rank among
princesses after the future reigning Empress. He
proposed to keep her near him, as his best and
most loving friend."

On the 15th of December, the great sacrifice
was finally consummated. In the Emperor's
cabinet were assembled Napoleon, Josephine,
King Louis, King Jerome, King Murat, the
Queens of Spain, Naples, Holland, and Westphalia, Napoleon's mother, his sister Pauline, and
Prince Eugene. Napoleon, with tears in his eyes,
explained to the princely family gathered together
the political necessity of his divorce. Speaking
of Josephine, he said with a touching emotion and
absolute sincerity : —

" She has embellished fifteen years of my life, the remembrance of which will remain for ever engraved on my heart. She was crowned by my hand, and I desire that she shall preserve the rank and the title of Empress, but, above all, that she never doubt my sentiments, and that she look upon me always as her best and dearest friend."

After Napoleon's words, Josephine made an effort to reply to the Emperor's declaration. Alas! notwithstanding all her efforts at self-control, long and frequent sobs strangled her utterances.

Comte Regnault de Saint-Jean d'Angély, who held the position of Officer of Civil State for the imperial family, was obliged to come to her assistance, and in a flood of tears, her voice broken by sobs, she said, —

" With the permission of my august and beloved husband, I owe it to him to declare that, having no hope of having children who could satisfy the needs of his policy and the interests of France, I am glad to be able to give him the greatest proof of affection and devotion which any woman on earth has ever given. I owe everything to his bounty; his hand crowned me, and from the height of this throne I have always received proofs of affection and love from the French people.

" I believe I understand his sentiments in consenting

to the dissolution of a marriage which is an obstacle to the welfare of France, which deprives it of the good fortune of being one day governed by the descendants of a great man so evidently raised up by Providence to obliterate the evils of a terrible revolution, and re-establish the church, the throne, and social order. But the dissolution of this marriage will never change the sentiments of my heart. The Emperor will always have in me his best friend. I know how this act, demanded of him by politics and his great interest, has racked his heart, but both of us glory in the sacrifice we are making for our country."

Napoleon tenderly embraced Josephine for the last time in her life, and led her half fainting to her children's arms.

What poignant emotions must have been Eugene's during this never-to-be-forgotten scene! All was not finished for him, however, and he must drink the bitter chalice to the dregs. The Senate, called together in solemn session, pronounced the dissolution of the marriage, — fatal sentence, which not only was the Prince constrained to hear, but to which he was obliged to reply in his mother's name, that of his sister, and his own. In a firm, manly voice and a noble modesty and touching simplicity, which deeply moved the assembly, he expressed himself in the following words: —

" My mother, my sister, and myself owe everything to the Emperor. To my sister and myself he has been a real father, and he will find in us for ever devoted children.

" It is necessary to the glory of France that the founder of the Fourth Dynasty should grow old surrounded by direct heirs, who will be our guarantee to all as a pledge for the glory of our country.

" When our mother was crowned before the whole nation, by the hands of her august husband, she contracted the obligation to sacrifice her affections to the interests of France. She has fulfilled the first of these duties with courage, nobility, and dignity. Her heart has often been touched in seeing the heart of this man, accustomed to commanding fortune and marching firmly forward to the accomplishment of his designs, the prey to melancholy longings for a direct heir. The tears which this resolution has cost the Emperor are recompense enough for my mother ! "

The French Senate, though devoted to Napoleon, was so moved by Prince Eugene's speech, and so touched by his noble attitude, that some members moved to send a deputation to carry their condolences to the Prince; but other members observed that such a step might be misinterpreted. A large number of the senators went singly and presented their condolences. Visitors of all kinds flocked to the Viceroy. The most

touching as well as the most honourable interest
was manifested in his welfare.

The next day, Eugene accompanied Josephine
to Malmaison.

"It had been decided upon in advance," as
Mademoiselle Avrillon relates on this subject,
"that, the day after the divorce, Their Majesties
should leave Paris, — the Emperor for Trianon,
the Empress for Malmaison. From early morning
of our last day at the Tuileries, we were all astir,
to lend what aid we each could to the preparations necessary for a departure which was for ever.
I remained in the Empress's apartments for a
long time, helping to pack her belongings: her
children were with her; they never left her.
Prince Eugene forced himself to appear at ease
and affected a brave mien; he even tried to force
a gaiety which was far from his heart."

At last the inexorable hour of departure
sounded, and Josephine crossed the threshold of
the Tuileries for the last time. Dethroned sovereign, banished wife, she left for ever this place
which she had entered in a blaze of glory to share
a throne, the most brilliant, perhaps, upon which
any woman had ever sat. With what a flood of
distressing thoughts this broken heart was overwhelmed!

Eugene's place after those days of agony was near his mother, and he remained at Malmaison. Sad, indeed, were the first hours passed by Josephine in that dear spot hallowed by such sweet memories!

Mademoiselle Avrillon writes of them thus:

"The first day, but especially the first night, was extremely painful. The Empress was plunged in deep affliction, but Her Majesty was not ill. I remained near her the greater part of the night. Sleep was impossible, and time passed as we conversed sadly. A great grief held her in its grasp. No doubt she deplored her fate, but in such sweet terms, in so resigned a manner, that everything which has been said to the contrary is pure invention. No bitterness entered into her discourse, even during this first night, in which the blow which had struck her was so recent; she spoke of the Emperor with the same respect and the same affection as in the past."

Eugene displayed during these sorrowful happenings a loftiness of soul which did not belie for one instant the abnegation and calm serenity which are found in this letter to his wife:—

PARIS, December 16, 1809.

It was impossible for me to write to you yesterday, my dear Augusta, as I remained with the Empress until midnight. At last this separation between the Emperor and my mother, which has been a subject of conversation with the public for so long a time, has been an accomplished fact since yesterday evening. A family gathering was held at the Tuileries. The Emperor explained the reasons which necessitated the step he had taken, of separating from his wife, and commanded the sacrifice; the Empress replied with nobility and dignity and with the most touching sensibility. The Arch-Chancellor drew up the *procès-verbal* of the *séance*, and we all signed it.

This morning, I repaired to a special meeting of the Senate; and, carrying out the Emperor's wishes, I explained the sentiments which had animated my family in these circumstances. Everything passed quietly, and the Empress displayed the greatest courage and resignation. To-morrow or the day after, a full account of the proceedings will be published in the papers, and you will see it. The Emperor goes to Trianon, the Empress to Malmaison, and I set out at once to rejoin you. Adieu, my very dear Augusta; I love you and my two little ones beyond any words.

At that moment, when Eugene, upon leaving the senate-chamber, penned the foregoing lines from Paris to the Princess, she wrote the following words, so full of noble resignation, as though their thoughts were mingled through the realms of space in a common sentiment of heroic abnegation, placed high above human illusions: —

· MILAN, December 16, 1809.

I am resigned to everything, and submit myself to the will of God; your greatness of soul may astonish many, but not your wife, who loves you, if such a thing is possible, more than ever. I will prove to you, dear Eugene, that I have not less courage or strength of character than you have, though I was forced to be far from you during these sad events. The little ones are well; God knows what their future will be.

Adieu, best of husbands; remember that my only desire is to do what you would wish me to, and to give you proofs of my tenderness, which will only end with the life of your faithful wife.

This letter had barely time to cross the Alps before Eugene seemed to anticipate it, he had so much faith in his wife's goodness of heart, which he knew he possessed entirely.

The day after his arrival at Malmaison he wrote as follows: —

MALMAISON, December 17, 1809.

We have been at Malmaison since yesterday evening, my very dear Augusta. If the weather had been better, we should have passed a more cheerful day; but it has poured ever since we arrived. The Empress is well. Her grief was very acute this morning, upon seeing once more, under such sad circumstances, the spots where she had passed so many happy days with the Emperor; but she soon regained her courage, and is, in a measure, resigned to her new position. For my

part, I firmly believe she will become happier and
more tranquil.

We received several visits this morning. Every one
is speaking, so they tell us, in Paris of our courage and
the Empress's resignation. They would be fools who
believed for one moment that I regretted any favour or
elevation. I hope, by the manner in which I bowed to
circumstances, I shall convince even the most incredu-
lous that I am above all that. I will not hide from
you that, during all these miserable days, I have had
but one worry, and that was that this event would cause
you sorrow. You should have seen a full account of
this affair in the *Moniteur* of this morning; I hope to
be in Milan soon, and then you will tell me frankly
what you think of the whole matter.

A week passed, and Josephine's grief, though
still great, was not so poignant. A visit from
Napoleon seemed to have solaced her a little;
and Eugene appeared sensible of the kindness
shown his mother by the Emperor: —

MALMAISON, December 26, 1809.

MY DEAR AUGUSTA, — The Emperor came to see
the Empress day before yesterday. Yesterday she
went to Trianon to see him, and he kept her to dinner.
The Emperor was very kind and affectionate to her,
and she seems better in consequence. Everything leads
me to think the Empress will be much happier in her
new position, and we also. You may believe me, as I
view the matter impartially. I hope your health has not

suffered in consequence of these new circumstances, and I beg of you to compose yourself. There is nothing to regret, and we shall always be happy because we shall always love each other.

Augusta's letters to her husband were for the latter a source of consolation in this crisis in which the future of the Beauharnais was threatened with disaster. Each of the Vice-Queen's letters testified more strongly to her strength of character, her indifference to the greatness now for ever lost, and her boundless love for the chivalrous husband of whom she was so proud. Their mutual affection was fostered in these cruel trials; and in all truth Eugene could write December 28 : —

My dear Augusta, — You are very good and very loving to write me the charming letters which I have received. I am very happy in knowing you approve of my conduct in this affair. For me, I am proud to be your husband, and I love you a hundred times more than I ever imagined I possibly could do.

VI.

The world has shown itself curious as to the relations between Napoleon and the dethroned Empress during the first days following the divorce. Constant enlightens us fully on this subject when he tells us that each time he re-

turned to Paris with the Emperor, he no sooner
arrived than he was sent to Malmaison. He
rarely carried a letter from the Emperor, who
only wrote to Josephine on very special occa-
sions. "Say to the Empress that I am well, and
that I desire her to be happy." That is what His
Majesty generally said to him as he saw him setting out.

As soon as he arrived, the Empress left every
one to talk to him. He often remained an hour,
and sometimes even two hours, during these
times. The sole subject of conversation was the
Emperor. Constant must tell her all Napoleon
had suffered while travelling, and if he had been
sad or gay, ill or well. She wept over the details given her, making a thousand suggestions
for the Emperor's health and the care she wished
given him.

Prince Eugene prolonged his visit to his
mother until she was somewhat reconciled to her
sad fate. Not only the new year 1810 found him
beside Josephine, but the month of January and
part of February passed before he found it possible to leave her.

On the 7th of February, the Princess, whose
tender impatience to clasp her beloved husband

in her arms became stronger day by day, wrote
a letter which is so charming, and which so exactly depicts the strength of the tie which united
these loving hearts, that I give it in full.   I only
wish to explain that the allusion made to the fate
reserved by Napoleon for the Viceroy concerned
the Grand Duchy of Frankfort, in connection
with which Eugene's name had been already
mentioned : —

MILAN, February 7, 1810.

The King of Naples availed himself of another
route, notwithstanding it had been announced that he
intended to pass through Milan.   I hope he will learn
that everything was prepared to give him a reception
befitting his rank as King.   I flatter myself, my dear
friend, that you will not follow his example, but will
take the shortest route possible to come here.   You
ought to know the pleasure your arrival will give me
and all the kingdom, whose uneasiness grows in measure
as your absence is prolonged.   I have been very careful
not to speak of the Grand Duchy.   Any indiscretion
on my part would have given rise to a general alarm.
Our people have proved how much they love us in
this last matter.   The Emperor could not possibly be
angry with us, for we have not intrigued for that; and
our way of thinking has always been, and always will
be, the same.   I do not believe, to tell you the truth,
in the fate in store for us; but our confidence should
indemnify us for a forgetfulness which without that

would be painful, and which you only inflict upon yourself on my account. But do you not know me, my
dear husband, and do you not know that with you and
my dear children I should always be happy? I am
young, but recent events have taught me to appreciate
the real value of greatness. Thus, do not worry yourself on my account, and only think of the happiness
which will be mine when I can tell you that I love
nothing in this world as I do my Eugene, and that this
sentiment will last as long as I live.

At last Eugene set out for Milan. He entered
the city after an absence of two months and a
half, February 18, 1810. The elevation of his
sentiments, the nobility of his heart, of which he
gave proof in all the painful details of the divorce,
are beyond all praise ; and few men of his age
would have been capable of them. I have already
said that, since his marriage with the Princess of
Bavaria, Napoleon's promises had given him the
right to consider himself heir presumptive to the
Crown of Italy, and even the eventual heir to
the imperial throne.

This last opinion is confirmed by Baron Sarcey,
who was in a position to judge of the strained
relations of Napoleon with several members of
his family.

Eugene's eventual right was to succeed the

Emperor, in default of a direct heir, and after those of Napoleon's brothers. Joseph, the oldest, was but thirteen years older than Josephine's son. Louis was very sickly and ill adapted for a ruler. Lucien, on account of his marriage with the widow Jouberthon, besides other complications, had become estranged from Napoleon. Besides, the Emperor often had occasion to complain of his brothers. Nobody was ignorant of the fact that he often went so far as to threaten them with disgrace in order to prevent them from carrying out some totally unfit policy. Joseph was on such bad terms with him, and carried it to such an extent, that the King of Spain absented himself from the ceremonies of the divorce, and shortly afterwards refused to be present at the marriage with Marie Louise, — a hostile attitude which greatly aroused Napoleon's anger.

These dissensions in the bosom of the imperial family greatly augmented the chances which seemed to promise a brilliant future to Eugene. Madame Bonaparte was herself of this opinion, as Baron Sarcey, in his admirable book, the *Mother of Napoleon*, tells us : —

"Madame Mère, who held the Empress's son in high esteem, saw in him a direct successor to Napoleon, in default of one of his brothers, to his imperial throne."

*Maria Letizia Ramolino (Madame Bonaparte),
Mother of the Emperor.*

One can easily see what an immense sacrifice was imposed on the young Viceroy by the divorce and second marriage. It was the double throne which Eugene saw vanishing into thin air. And what a throne! But this resplendent prospect, which would have dazzled any other than this Prince, had glided by without leaving any impression on the unshaken modesty which was one of the most beautiful traits of his character.

On his return to Milan, Eugene, far from displaying any animosity towards the Emperor for the loss of such brilliant prospects, consecrated himself with more zeal than ever to the cares of his kingdom, which had been enlarged by the annexation of a portion of the Tyrol, and now numbered 6,500,000 inhabitants.

A week had hardly elapsed since his return and his taking up of the reins of government, when Napoleon made a formal announcement to him of his coming marriage with the Archduchess Louise. To complete the irony of a cruel fate, three days later a second letter reached him in which he received orders to repair to Paris to assist at the betrothal of his adopted father with the woman who was so soon to occupy the place of a tenderly loved mother.

PARIS, February 26, 1810.

MY SON, — The Emperor of Austria having acceded
to my demands for the hand of the Archduchess Marie
Louise, of whose merits and brilliant qualities I am fully
cognisant, I have resolved to fix the date of our marriage in Paris for the 29th of March. I have sent the
Prince de Neuchatel to assist as my witness at the
marriage ceremony, which will take place, March 6,
at Vienna, by proxy, to enable the Empress to reach
Compiègne the 23d, where I expect to meet her.
At this important event I have determined to gather
around me all the princes and princesses of my family,
and I now advise you by this letter to allow no impedi-
ment to prevent you from being in Paris by the 20th
of March.

Thus Eugene, after having seen his mother,
not two months before, descend from the greatest
throne in the world, was obliged to assist with a
still bleeding heart at the elevation of the woman
who was to succeed her.

CHAPTER V.

Prince Eugene refuses the Throne of Sweden. — Family Life.
— Birth of the King of Rome. — Eugene is summoned by
Napoleon. — Rupture with the Czar. — The Crown of Poland.
— Eugene resolves to refuse it, if it be offered to him. — Pros-
pects of Peace. — War is declared.

I.

FAITHFUL to the promise which he had
made officially in a message addressed to
the Senate at the time of the divorce, assuring
Eugene's future, Napoleon named him heir to
the Grand Duchy of Frankfort. This nomination
was accompanied by the most flattering eulogies
of the Prince. The following is an extract
from the message, published in the *Moniteur* of
March 4, 1810: —

"It is with loving eagerness that our heart prompts
us on this occasion to give a new proof of our esteem
and great affection for a young Prince whose first steps
in governing and in the army were taken under our
direction; and who, in the midst of varied circumstances,
has never given us the slightest cause for discontent, but

who, on the contrary, has seconded our efforts with a
prudence far above what could be expected from his
age, and in this last campaign has displayed at the head
of our armies as much bravery as knowledge of the art
of war. It pleases us to establish him firmly in the
high rank in which we have placed him."

But what solace were these praises and the
expression of this satisfaction to Eugene, who
found himself obliged to assist at the ceremony
which was a death-blow to his filial love? Napoleon's marriage to Marie Louise was set for
March 29. On the 12th, the Viceroy and his wife
set out for Paris, where they arrived on the 20th.
At that time the journey from Milan to Paris
occupied eight days. At first they took up their
residence in the Palace of the Elysée, from which,
forty years later, one of their nephews was to set
out to assume again the imperial purple.

The Princess had hardly reached Paris when
her tender heart urged her to hasten to Malmaison to embrace Josephine. She intuitively
divined how consoling and soothing her presence
would be to the Empress. The Vice-Queen,
during her protracted sojourn, occupied an adjoining apartment to those devoted to Josephine's
use; and these two women, so different in their

characters, yet both sweet-tempered, good, sensitive, and united by a common tie, their love for Eugene, spent long, delicious hours together, — hours precious to bleeding hearts. Augusta's presence was a consolation which Josephine appreciated more fully for the reason that she was soon to exile herself to her château at Navarre near Evreux, so as not to be a drawback to the festivities inaugurated to celebrate the Emperor's second marriage.

During the Empress's sojourn at Navarre, Eugene paid her several visits; regarding these visits, I have found some very interesting notes, which contain a faithful portrait of Eugene at that time : —

"It was impossible to imagine more amiability and good-fellowship than belonged to the Viceroy; to captivate his associates, he put himself out to be as amiable and agreeable as an humble individual of no special rank. A declared enemy to etiquette, he tried to avoid it here as much as possible; he forbade the hussars to announce him, in order to spare us the trouble of rising each time he entered. 'It is bad enough,' he said, 'to be forced to submit to these tiresome consequences of etiquette when I am in Milan; at least permit me to amuse myself a little here. It is a hard trade to be a king, when one has not been brought up to it!' I have

seen him at Malmaison, crossing the garden in a pour-
ing rain, to avoid the ceremonious announcement which
his appearance in the gallery would entail.

" His fine, delicate face lighted up in an extraordinary
manner when speaking of his campaigns. His carriage
was noble and elegant, and he never came without be-
stowing numerous gifts; and, as Josephine remarked
with all a mother's pride, every one's face lighted up
with happiness on seeing him. No son could show
such a filial love and at the same time such fatherly
protection towards an unhappy mother. He could
never speak of the period of his mother's divorce
without tears in his eyes."

During the Viceroy's stay in Paris, Napoleon,
desirous of compensating him in every possible
manner for the overthrow of the hopes his second
marriage had ruined, conceived a step of twofold
importance, in an historical point of view and as
showing the disinterestedness of my hero's character. He sent Duroc, Marshal of the Palace, to
offer him the Crown of Sweden. The Swedes,
who, on one side, wanted to assure the succession
to their childless King, Charles XII., and, on the
other, felt the necessity of placing over their government, in those troubled times, a man who had
been tried and found worthy, had with this end
in view made overtures to Napoleon's Court.

They justly argued that among these princes
and French marshals they would find an heir
worthy of sustaining the splendour of the throne
of Gustavus Adolphus and Charles XII.

Baron Darnay, in his Memoirs. thus describes
this curious incident : —

" In the midst of the bustle of the wedding *fêtes*, the
Emperor sent the Marshal of the Palace, Duroc, to the
Viceroy, then living at the Palace of the Elysée, to offer
him, in his name, the throne of Sweden.   The Marshal, an old friend of Eugene's, employed all his persuasive powers, strengthened by his attachment to the
Prince, to induce Eugene to concede to the Emperor's
wish.   The Viceroy asserted that he was perfectly contented with his present destiny in Italy; and that he
feared he would not be able to gain the esteem of a
people for whom he had done nothing.   The Prince
ended by begging Marshal Duroc to return his thanks
and his respectful regrets to the Emperor.

" The next day, the Marshal reappeared on the part
of the Emperor, and insisted, in His Majesty's name,
upon Eugene's reconsidering the proposition of the previous day; he remarked to the Prince that the kingdom
of Italy, in the event of two imperial sons, would pass
to the second; that the Prince, by his fame as a warrior,
could hardly fail to please a brave, warlike nation; and
that the virtues of the Princess Augusta would be appreciated and would gladden all hearts.

" The Viceroy, having had all that day and the day

before to confer with the Vice-Queen, who shared her husband's opinion, persisted in his resolutions to take all the chances of his position; and he renewed his thanks to the Emperor, praying Marshal Duroc to carry him his most respectful excuses.

"The Emperor remarked to the Viceroy that same day that he might perhaps be right, and that he had no ill-will towards him, dropping the subject from that day forth."

It was so evidently to Napoleon's interest to throw the weight of his influence in favour of one of the princes of his family, or of a man whom he knew to be entirely devoted to him, that his most natural choice fell on Eugene, and for a moment the latter's refusal caused him great annoyance. This throne finally fell in 1818 to Marshal Bernadotte, who ascended it under the name of Charles XIV. (Charles Jean).

What influenced Eugene most, perhaps, was the fact that he would be obliged to change his religion before mounting the steps of this throne. In regard to this refusal of Eugene's, Metternich cites these significant words of Napoleon in the course of a conversation on this delicate subject: —

"'The choice of the Prince de Ponte-Corvo (Bernadotte) presents points of view which are very disagreeable to me,' the Emperor remarked: ' it compromises my relations with Russia, and places another man out of private life on a throne, which is an injury to royalty. The question of a change of religion is not an indifferent one either, if we can judge by the effect of this news on the Empress Marie Louise. She cried out on hearing it, " What! this coward gives up his God for a crown?" Thank God none of mine were guilty of that! I offered the crown to the Viceroy of Italy, who refused it point-blank.' "

This definitely settles the fact that the Crown of Sweden was offered to Eugene, — a fact testified to by a witness worthy of all confidence. Here are the words of a more recent authority :

"Napoleon placed so little confidence in Bernadotte that he pondered over a more suitable French candidate, and proposed Prince Eugene to the Swedes, who were asking for Bernadotte. Eugene was approached, but not being willing to change his religion, which was an indispensable condition for reigning at Stockholm, he was forced to return to Prince de Ponte-Corvo, who was not troubled in the slightest degree by the same scruples."

It is certain that Eugene's election, as Napoleon's adopted son, a ruler whose wisdom and worth had been proven by Italy, would have been easier than that of Bernadotte, who was far from possessing the same prestige and presenting the same guarantees. One word from the Emperor would have been sufficient to have made the Swedes declare in Eugene's favour, while they, on the other hand, in choosing the Prince de Ponte-Corvo, imagined they were pleasing Napoleon. As we have seen, this choice displeased the latter, especially as it compromised his relations with the Czar.

As this is more a romance of Prince Eugene's life than his political history, no further importance need be attached to this fact than the new light it throws upon the character of one whom Thiers, that great national historian in his chapter on Napoleon's divorce, calls, "the excellent Prince." An ambitious man, anxious to grasp a sceptre, would he not have hastened to accept the offer made him? Would he not have intrigued and moved heaven and earth to make himself the choice of the Swedes? Does not this short, decisive refusal, at the very first overtures, prove the sincerity of Eugene's modesty, and show that he only regretted Italy's crown for the sake of his wife and children? This kingdom of Italy, whose reorganisation had been his pride, was made for his pleasure. He would have preferred to reign under its bright blue sky, over a people who had learned to love him, rather than, putting the question of religion to one side, to bury himself in an inhospitable climate, so far from his own land and that of his wife. But I think that neither the throne of France of which his wife had dreamed, nor the Crown of Italy to which he had legal rights, nor the sceptre of Sweden which Napoleon had offered him, nor the purple of Poland which was in question, dazzled him for one moment. Eugene had enough experience of life to know that happiness is not a privilege of the great, and that a destiny in a lower scale, the love of a cherished wife and the sweet affection of his children, added to the esteem and consideration of the world, constituted enviable happiness on this earth.

Besides, by a sort of providence, his children, for whom alone he was ambitious, later mounted the steps of a throne or were allied with royal houses. This same Crown of Sweden, which Eugene had disdained, was afterwards worn by one of his daughters, the wife of Charles XV., Bernadotte's son.

The Prince and Princess took part in all the *fêtes* attending the imperial marriage, and pro-

longed their stay in France until the month of
May. They were present at the *fête* given by
the Prince de Schwarzenberg, which has gone
down to history famous for the frightful conflagration which engulfed so many illustrious victims.
Here, again, Eugene's star appeared to protect
him by its mysterious power. The Viceroy had
opened the ball with Princess Pauline de Schwarzenberg, wife of the ambassador's elder brother.
When the catastrophe broke forth, he found
himself, happily for him, a little to one side and
behind the crowd. A chandelier fell, and the
platform, blazing up, barred his passage. By a
providential chance he discovered a little door
leading to the private apartments of the hotel,
and was thus enabled to penetrate to where the
Princess was, and save her before she gained any
knowledge of her peril. He not only saved her
from harm, but also spared her any fright, because she knew nothing of the danger she had
escaped until she was clear of it.

II.

It was June before the royal couple returned
to Italy. The Empress Josephine, who was at
Aix, joined them later at Monza, where Eugene

at once plunged with renewed ardour into the administrative labours of his kingdom.

Eugene and his wife passed several happy months in their country home, enjoying a homely family life. During these few months spent in the company of his wife and children, he laboured ceaselessly. He kept up a constant correspondence with Napoleon.

It does not enter into the plan of this work to give this political and administrative correspondence. I think it sufficient to mention that the Viceroy's indefatigable activity extended to every branch of his government. He laboured to enlarge the army and navy, in the development of public works and commerce, in erecting numerous hospitals, in perfecting his fortifications, in establishing a just system of taxation, and in general in protecting all the interests of the country which were necessary. His hardest task was his struggle against the inroads of English commerce and the successful defence of his kingdom against Napoleon's oftentimes arbitrary demands.

December 9, 1810, the happiness of the Viceroy was completed by the birth of a son: Auguste Charles Eugene Napoleon, who in 1834 wedded Donna Maria da Gloria, Queen of Portugal.

The birth of this child was a signal for universal rejoicings throughout the kingdom; for the people, *bourgeoisie* and nobility alike, were animated by a common affection for Eugene and his wife.

Their joy would have been much more exuberant if the fatal divorce had not modified Napoleon's plans with regard to Eugene, and if the little Prince who had just been born could have been looked upon as the future heir to the Crown of Italy.

During the year 1811, Europe enjoyed a profound peace, which gave no warnings of the disasters of the Russian campaign. This happy but too short truce gave Eugene an opportunity to put some of the numerous plans which he had been nursing for the good of his people into execution. He organised the Institute of Sciences at Milan, with branches in Venice, Bologna, Padua, and Verona; he endowed and maintained several special academies, and at Milan founded a college for young girls, with the end in view of encouraging flax-raising, — one of the most important industries in his kingdom; he offered a prize of a million francs for the invention of the best machine for spinning flax.

But all his happy and peaceful innovations came to a standstill.

Napoleon had at first intended to undertake his campaign against Russia in the spring of 1811; and in order that Italy should be ready to place at his disposal the great number of men he demanded of her, he had ordered Eugene to equip a powerful army before the month of May, 1811. The organising of these troops claimed the Viceroy's incessant attention. Thanks to the postponement of this fatal campaign, which was destined to engulf the largest number of men ever collected, and prepare the insidious over-throw of the imperial throne, Eugene was en-abled, during the greater part of the year, to enjoy the felicity of his fireside.

A command from Napoleon interrupted the conjugal happiness of the young couple for several weeks. He demanded the presence of the Viceroy at Paris, when, to his great joy, Marie Louise gave birth to the ardently longed for child; though instead of the promised crowns, fate reserved exile and premature death for the young orphan, crushed under the overwhelming greatness of a name which, long after the down-fall of the giant, still possessed the power to make Europe tremble.

Napoleon wished Eugene himself to announce the birth of the little King of Rome to Josephine. Painful as this delicate mission must have been, Eugene obeyed with his usual noble simplicity.

" The Viceroy assured Josephine that the Emperor had said to him as he took leave of him: ' You are going to see your mother, Eugene; tell her that I am sure she will rejoice with me in my happiness more than any one else. I should have written to her before, if I had not been absorbed in the pleasure of gazing at my son. I only tear myself away from him to attend to the most indispensable duties. This evening I will discharge the sweetest of them all, — I shall write to Josephine.' "

During Eugene's stay in France, Napoleon and he talked long and earnestly on the Italian army, which in the following year was to carry the tricolour into the depths of Russia. Thanks to his constant and energetic efforts, Eugene stood ready, at the end of 1811, to march at the head of fifty thousand men and five thousand horses.

One of the principal causes of the disastrous campaign which was about to commence was this ill-omened Austrian marriage, upon which Napoleon had counted to consolidate his greatness and which — as if Providence had wished to avenge the repudiated wife — was the origin of his downfall.

Napoleon had decided, in order to strengthen his dynasty, to contract a second marriage, and hesitated a long time between an archduchess of Austria, and the Grand-Duchess Anne of Russia, a sister to the Emperor Alexander. His first choice had fallen on the latter, but difficulties arose at once. The Empress-Mother disapproved of the marriage, urging the extreme youth of her daughter as an excuse. Alexander, on his side, owing to the reputed coldness springing up between France and Russia, showed little haste to reply to Napoleon's advances, and matters dragged along. Was this slowness, in exhausting the patience of the master of France, the true reason for the failure of this marriage project? This would be rather a foolhardy assertion to make. On the other hand, Alexander, it cannot be denied, was very jealous of the creation of the Grand Duchy of Warsaw which Napoleon bestowed on his ally, the King of Saxony; according to Thiers, the Czar, seeing in the formation of this new State the menace of a reconstruction of the old kingdom of Poland, exacted as the price of his consent to a marriage with his sister the secret and formal promise on the part of the all-powerful Pretender never to reorganise the obliterated kingdom. But M. Vandal, thanks to recent researches, has been able to establish, in an irrefutable manner, the fact that, though consenting to sign such a convention, Napoleon did not obtain the hand of the Grand-Duchess, and that Alexander's parleyings, agreeing with the Empress-Mother's, were in reality but pretexts.

In the mean while, Austria, in the grasp of the iron hand of the conqueror, declared herself ready to " sacrifice " (this was the term employed by the Emperor Francis himself) an archduchess. Napoleon, annoyed by the repeated delays of Russia, put an end to Alexander's parleys with his accustomed brusqueness.

This violent rupture fermented the difficulties pending between the courts of Paris and St. Petersburg on the subject of Poland, the continual stumbling-block of the Duchy of Oldenburg, and other questions of too complex a nature to be mentioned here. If it cannot be said to be the direct and determining cause of the war, it can be safely looked upon as being at least the secondary and indirect cause.

Beyond doubt, if Napoleon had not divorced himself, the political difficulties, not being embittered by the personal resentments between the two Emperors, would have been capable of an easier solution. Unhappily the self-love of both was wounded, — Napoleon's by the subterfuges of Alexander, who pretended to shelter himself behind his mother's wishes ; that of Alexander by the impolite manner in which Napoleon broke off negotiations before the true meaning of his secret decision was officially announced.

III.

At the beginning of 1812, Eugene was placed in command of the Fourth Army Corps, composed of Italians, and the Sixth Corps (Bavarians), making a total of eighty thousand soldiers, who set out the 16th of February. In order to enable this army to cross the Alps, it was necessary to clear the gorges of Brenner of the enormous masses of snow by which they were obstructed, and which rendered the passage almost impracticable. These difficult operations were organised and executed with the greatest secrecy, as Napoleon feared that Russia, divining the destination of this army, would invade the Grand Duchy of Warsaw and Old Prussia, which the great general wished to keep free as a basis for his operations.

A few days before leaving Milan, Eugene informed his relative and intimate friend, the Comte de la Valette, of his assuming command. I cite this letter because it shows at once how little ambition Eugene had for a throne.

The rumour had spread that the real cause of the war was the desire which Napoleon nursed to punish Russia by re-establishing the ancient kingdom of Poland, in order to bestow it on Eugene. This is the letter on that subject which the latter wrote to the Comte de la Valette : —

MILAN, February 22, 1812.

At last my fate is decided: I have received a grand command, and though it is not yet publicly given out, I am at liberty to announce it to you.   I command the Fourth Corps of the Army and that of the Bavarians, which they say Saint-Cyr commands.   You can easily see that this will give me from seventy thousand to eighty thousand men and nearly two hundred pieces of cannon.

The generals, officers, and soldiers, who have just come from Paris, assure me that it is said I shall be placed in command of the cavalry.   In any case I shall be well placed, and any position which leaves me at liberty to give the greatest number of proofs of absolute devotion to His Majesty will be the post I shall always prefer.

One thing does not make me feel any too much pleased.   That is the rumour which calls my unworthy self to Poland.   This rumour has been spread here; and

I assure you it has given me real sorrow. I could not live so far from the Emperor; my sole ambition is to live and die as near to him as possible. You will tell me that I am not hard to please, and you are right. I am not devoid of ambition; but I have not the ambition which aspires to thrones, that is certain, as it is also certain that I have a lifelong friendship for you.

If the young Viceroy of Italy evinced little desire for the Crown of Poland, such was far from being the case with the Poles in regard to (as he modestly says) "his unworthy self." They ardently longed for him at Warsaw, where they nursed the hope of seeing the armies of France raise up Poland's fallen greatness. I desire no greater proof of this than these lines, addressed a few months later to Eugene, who had just reached the shores of the Niemen, by General Rosinkwi, one of the most illustrious men of his country: —

"All the people of Poland, without one exception, are expressing wishes which I can feel and share better with the nation than I should know how to explain to Your Imperial Highness. To-day you are the only person who commands our suffrages, and on you alone our eyes are cast. We dare not defy the Emperor's will; but the Emperor himself cannot prevent our hearts from feeling for Your Imperial Highness that of which reason would not disapprove. It may be possible I offend the nobility of Your Imperial Highness by these words; it is also possible I may be too bold in daring to broach this topic. If such is the case, I will promise to be silent in the future, or until occasion calls for it; but I cannot acknowledge myself in fault because I manifest the feelings with which my heart is filled, following the impression which our deep esteem for your noble character adds to all our hopes."

After an affecting farewell to his beloved wife and children, Eugene set out the 18th of April, in obedience to an urgent order from Napoleon to join him in Paris.

He remained a week in the French capital before joining his army. As though foreseeing the length of the separation and the frightful perils which he would be obliged to face, his heart dictated each day a new letter to the Princess, sometimes two in the same day. I shall not resist the pleasure of citing a few of them, of which the interest is great, whether it be from the perfume of tenderness which they exhale, or the bright light they throw upon the great events which were soon to unroll themselves before our eyes, — events in which Eugene was to take a part, which, in default of so many other claims, merits the admiration of posterity.

The Prince made the journey in four days from
Milan to Paris, which was exceptionally rapid
for that period. He did not find the Emperor
at the Tuileries. The latter, in truth, annoyed
by the low rumble of popular discontent which
reached his ears, had retired with his Court to
Saint-Cloud, the end of the previous month.
This man, who, having arrived at the pinnacle of
his astounding greatness and had only one more
fortunate campaign to make to hold the whole
Continent in his all-powerful hand, was obliged,
so to speak, to fly from the complaints of a people
hostile to the new war and groaning under the
weight of military taxes imposed by the glory of
the master they had themselves created.

Eugene reached Paris the 22d of April, and
after going to see the Emperor at Saint-Cloud,
to embrace his mother at Malmaison, he returned
to Paris in the evening worn out with fatigue.

IV.

The touching letter that follows contains the
pacific indications which were welcomed with
such avidity, at the moment previous to the
bursting forth of the most murderous war of

modern times. A word of explanation is here appropriate. The Russians, in the fear which Napoleon's overwhelming military genius inspired, had already mapped out their plan of the campaign. This consisted in destroying everything in advance of Napoleon, of leaving desolation in the path of his army in the hope of weakening its strength by famine and misery. In order to retard these devastations, at least until his army could concentrate itself in close proximity to the Slav frontiers, Napoleon not only manœuvred to keep the objective movements of his troops as secret as possible, but, with a most skilful duplicity, spread the rumour that peace was in a fair way not to be broken. The more imminent the war became, because his will rendered it inevitable, the more pronounced became his peaceful assurances.

The following letter from the Viceroy speaks of this certainty : —

PARIS, April 24, Midday.

Yesterday I received your first two letters, my good and loving Augusta, and they brought loving tears to my eyes. I never doubted your tenderness for me, but the assurances you give me in so touching a manner is very dear to me. Every member of the family whom I have seen up to the present moment has anxiously asked after you; and it gives me great pleasure to see that you are loved and appreciated as you deserve to be. I will no doubt astonish you in telling you that no one speaks of war here. A great many people, well informed, tell me that things may be arranged even yet.

A Russian officer, who passed day before yesterday through Metz, is awaited here to-day. Be tranquil, perfectly tranquil; do not alarm yourself. I advise you to this, and you should believe what I tell you. Do not doubt the loving tenderness which I have sworn for you for life. I embrace you and my little ones also. The Empress Marie is charmed with their portraits. I had the honour of making a hand at her game of whist yesterday, and she chatted most amicably about you and the details of our little household. I think it would be well for you to write to her.

Another letter, written two days afterwards, shows how sincere was his indifference in regard to royal dignities. His joy burst forth on learning that there was a question of King Jerome for Poland's throne: —

" I do not speak of the rumours of Paris, for it is in this city that they abound. For example, it is almost certain that the King of Westphalia will become the King of Poland. I give you this news especially, because you know how enchanted I shall be that there is nothing in it which concerns us; and I pray Heaven, which has cared for us so well, to leave us thus for the rest of our lives."

This short stay of the Viceroy's in Paris coincides with the most brilliant period of Napoleon's reign. With the campaign of Russia was really to commence the decadence of the most unique power in the world.

During these days, there were nothing but *fêtes* at the Court, in which Eugene took part with as happy a heart as his separation from his family permitted.

How many times, in after years, in his peaceful Bavarian retreat, living quietly in the bosom of his family, while Napoleon expiated so many triumphs on a rock lost in the middle of a far distant ocean, — how many times must his thoughts have gone back to those last dazzling days of this marvellous epoch, to which succeeded the shipwreck of the Empire !

In the midst of spectacles, hunting-parties, and amusements of all kinds, the rumours of peace were persistently reported by every mouth as the Emperor had willed, in order to mislead Russia completely. But Eugene's mind was too clairvoyant, his sagacity too keen, for him to be long carried away by this mirage.

"You must know that everything is wrapped in mystery here," he wrote, two days later, to the

Princess, " especially for those who, like me, seek
to know only what they are told."

On the 30th, Napoleon took him to Trianon
and Versailles, in his carriage: —

" I am waiting for my orders," he writes; " I
am more than ever like the bird on the branch."
And, terminating his letter in the loving language
habitual to him, he adds: " I embrace my little
angels; and, for their sake and mine, take good
care of your precious health."

V.

At last the hour sounded. Eugene received
his orders to join the army. This news could
not but greatly alarm an adored wife. Although
of a remarkable firmness of character, the Vice-
Queen was a sweet and loving woman. Why
should she not tremble at the announcement of
the war in which her beloved husband might
meet his death, as Lannes did, and so many of the
brave commanders of the army?

Notwithstanding all, Eugene could not dissimulate his joy at having, as he put it in his
own words, "a very fine command," — a soldier's
joy, who could only see in the horrors of war the
laurels to be gathered.

PARIS, May 1, 1812.

I announce the news to you, my dear Augusta, that the Emperor has ordered me to the front. I leave to-morrow morning. I have a very fine command under me, and am delighted to have the Bavarians with me. Do not worry over this news. Matters may still be arranged. Officers are coming and going between Paris and St. Petersburg; and it is stated there will be an interview between the two Emperors in which an understanding may be reached. But, above all things, do not worry. Count on my happiness; my lucky star will not abandon me, and everything is for the best. Embrace my children for me; I clasp you to my heart.

That same day Eugene wrote again to his wife. He feared she would suspect that he had deluded her with false hopes of peace, when he knew that war had been decided upon; and this sincere and loyal character could not endure the idea that, even in the smallest matters, the Princess should doubt his frankness : —

PARIS, May 1, 1812.

You must have been very much surprised at hearing of my hurried departure for the army; but I assure you it was very fortunate for me. One thing worried me greatly, and that is, that you might for a moment think I had misled you, and that I knew in advance I should join the army. You would do me a great injustice, my dear wife, for, I swear before God, I told you all I knew and the exact truth. I am anxious to know that you believe in my sincerity and also in my good fortune, which has doubled since we became united; and Heaven is too just not to continue its favours towards us. Adieu, my dearest Augusta. I shall be eight whole days in the carriage, without being able to write to you; but I shall write from Munich, and on every occasion which offers itself. Adieu, once more adieu.

He profited by a stop of two hours at Mayence to beg his wife not to worry and to take good care of herself. Brave heart, who, in the moment of facing the most formidable dangers, forgets himself to think of the tranquillity of the being whose happiness is more precious to him than his own life!

MAYENCE, May 5, 1812, 6 A.M.

I was obliged to make a halt at Mayence. My dear Augusta, I will profit by this delay to write you. I hope your health remains good, and that you will always be very careful of yourself for your children's sake and for love of me. This is the greatest proof of attachment you can give me. Adieu; I embrace you tenderly, and send many kisses to my little angels.

Still give me your love; it is the happiness of my life.

Six days' journey transported him from Paris to Dresden, where but a short while later the Emperor and Empress of Austria, the King of

Prussia, the King and Queen of Saxony, and so many German princes ran, like vassals at their sovereign's call, to offer Napoleon the incense of their homages, the supreme radiance of a dazzling greatness blazing up with greater brilliancy as it was about to be extinguished for ever. From Pilnitz, near Dresden, Eugene acquainted his wife with the charming reception accorded him by the royal family: —

PILNITZ, May 8, 1812, 11.30 P. M.

The King was very kind to me, the Queen charming. The Princess Augusta (the King's daughter) is very well; we talked of you a great deal, and I was made doubly happy as I listened to the justice which they rendered you. I shall not write to you again until I reach my headquarters; that is to say, amid the lands of Poland. Adieu, my good and very dear Augusta; my sentiments towards you will never change.

Each letter marked a new step, which carried him farther and farther from his loved ones, and nearer and nearer the theatre of war. Alas! each step also augmented the difficulty of receiving letters, the greatest suffering to those waiting and longing for them.

GLOGAU, May 11, 1812.

I hasten to announce my arrival at Glogau. I have had enough of being cooped up in a carriage for nine whole days. I have been on horseback all the morning, and have reviewed a good part of my troops. There will be many days that I shall be without news of you, my dear wife; and that saddens me, because I have contracted the pleasing habit of receiving your letters regularly. I shall have them more and more rarely now, but the safest way is to send your letters by the way of Paris. Adieu, my dear one; in a few days more I shall reach my destination, and I will then take up my pleasant task of giving you news of me often. Adieu; I embrace you as I love you, and my three little angels. Be careful of yourself, because you are necessary to all our happiness.

At last Eugene reached his headquarters on the Vistula. The sight of his Bavarian troops suggested a pretty compliment to the Princess, who, loyal Frenchwoman as she had become, still preserved a tender remembrance of her country in her heart: —

HEADQUARTERS AT PLOCK, May 15, 1812.

I am surrounded by Bavarians; but I do not need them to call to my mind that I possess what is most precious to them. I will pass them in review these dreary days, and shall hunt a little in the surrounding country.

Mon Dieu ! How far I am from you ! Do you know, that since the day I left you, a month has not passed, and yet it seems a century to me ! I have travelled nearly six hundred leagues.

The next day, the Viceroy, having finally received a letter from the Princess, wrote her, "I
am feeling very well, and much lighter in heart
and happier in mind since I have received news
of you."

Two days afterwards he mentioned the Emperor's departure; and, in his desire to hasten
the conquest of a glorious peace, he cried out, in
the tones of a young general intoxicated with the
roar of the cannons, "So much the better: the
sooner it commences, the sooner it will be finished, and the sooner I shall find myself again in
your arms."

In another letter, he mentions the cleverness
with which Napoleon had kept Alexander in
doubt as to his warlike intentions, and exclaimed
gaily, "Do you know, there are many people
who still do not believe in the war?"

The nearer Eugene approached the battle-fields
of the future, the more he endeavoured to inspire
the Princess with confidence and to make her a
sharer of the hopefulness of his own heart. "I
have told you, and I repeat," he writes, "that
nothing could have made me happier than being
sent to the front; I am very happy to be here.
Do not worry about me, for I rely on my good
star."

Though on the point of engaging in battle on the Russian steppes, nothing could turn his thoughts from Italy and the loving companion he had left behind him. Although the Princess's birthday was still far away, he had thought of it: "As I fear my despatches may be detained *en route*, I have this day sent you a little birthday present by way of Paris; I am anxious that it should reach you in time. There are still twenty-two days."

Could anything be more touching than these simple words; and how could the Princess help being touched to the bottom of her heart? Eugene returns to the subject again in the following note: —

SOLDAU, June 6, 1812.

Here I am at Soldau, my dear Augusta; the guard arrived here this morning. The army is so grand and so enthusiastic that it leads me to hope the war will not last over the winter. It will be so sweet to feel your dear arms around me again, before the bitter cold reaches us. Your birthday falls in this month; it will not be the first I have passed away from you, but my heart is near you at present, and I assure you it is impossible to love you more than I do now.

Unhappily this correspondence, after becoming more and more rare as the distance lengthened, became day by day more uncertain. "Beg of the Duc de Lodi and Darnay," wrote Eugene from Sensburg, "to direct the despatch-couriers' route carefully, so that they may not fall into the hands of the Cossacks."

Provisions ran short not long afterwards, and long before hostilities commenced, the army suffered greatly.

"We are suffering for the necessities of life," the young general wrote from Rastenburg, under the date of June 14; "and this fact causes me many sleepless nights, when I think that I have eighty thousand men to feed every day, and oftentimes we cannot find ten bags of corn. But my consolation is that we are marching in advance of the harvest. I am very well, and want nothing but to hear from you oftener."

In the following letter, we find a new allusion to the desire of the Poles to have Eugene for their King, and a proof that the Princess shared her husband's aversion to the plan. Italy or nothing, — this was their common thought.

RASTENBURG, June 17, 1812.

MY DEAR AND GOOD AUGUSTA, — You may rest easy on the score of Poland; it is probable that the matter will be arranged without any reference to me. The Poles have made the most inconceivable overtures, but I have held to my first decision, and have not disguised the fact that they have pained me. It is certainly evident they are very anxious for me, and in proof of this I send you two letters which I have received from two of them; you need not show these to any one. They do not disguise the fact that they hope to have me for their King. At present I am almost positive it will arrange itself differently. We shall certainly pass our winter together, my dear Augusta, and this thought supports me through these dreary days. I am deeply sensible of my happiness, and I love you for it.

The 21st is the Vice-Queen's anniversary : —

"To-day is the 21st," the Prince writes; " and this is to say to you that I regret not being near you to-day more than other days, but my heart and my thoughts are never far from you."

At last the fatal moment arrives. Napoleon is about to cross the Niemen. June 24, Eugene writes : —

KALWARYA, June 24, 1812, Midday.

Bonjour, my dear, darling Augusta. I have just reached this place after marching all night. The guard arrived with me. To-morrow my entire corps will join me. To-day the Emperor is to cross the Niemen at several points.

The heat is something frightful, notwithstanding which I am very well. I love you, and shall love you all my life.

CHAPTER VI.

Campaign of Russia. — The Passage of the Niemen. — Sufferings of the Army from the Commencement of the Campaign. — Russian Tactics. — The Uneasiness of Absence. —
Napoleon as the Father of a Family. — The Battle of Moscow. — Prince Eugene's Glorious *Rôle* in this Battle. —
Entry into Moscow. — Incendiarism. — Uncertainty as to
the Future. — Overtures towards Peace. — The Order to
Retreat.

I.

I HAVE now arrived at the most painful as also
the most glorious epoch of Eugene's career.

Napoleon, in crossing the Niemen, had finally
thrown down the gauntlet to the Colossus of
the North.

The most sanguinary campaign in the annals
of history was about to commence. In the battle of Moscow alone, forty-seven generals were
lost. Eugene himself, intrepid soldier as he was
by nature, exposed his life to the chance of pay-
ing the forfeit from some flying bullet or ball,
and truly earned his reputation for bravery. On
those lugubrious fields of snow, white witnesses

of privations which no pen can paint, reddened
with the blood of hundreds of thousands of brave
men, he won a glorious reputation, ratified
by the judgment of Napoleon himself.

Before putting his foot on Russian soil, Eugene
had been obliged to undergo experiences spared
to the majority of the other generals. Instead
of crossing, as they did, Old Prussia, with its
cultivated fields and abundance of provisions, he
was obliged to open a route, at the price of innumerable privations, across the sterile wastes of
Poland. So long was he detained that when the
Grand Army entered Wilna, — Napoleon's first
halt in Russia, — Eugene had only just reached
the Niemen, which he crossed six days after the
Emperor.

His corps of the army had suffered terribly
during this astounding march of six hundred
leagues from the joyous plains of Italy to the
Muscovite frontiers. From the cruel effects of
a change of climate, unwholesome nourishment,
drought, lack of bread, of salt, and of wine, dysen-
tery had made such cruel ravages among the men
that, on reaching the Niemen, his main corps
of eighty thousand men was reduced to forty-
five thousand.

To superstitious minds, — and they were not lacking among the Italian troops, — the crossing of the river by the army was signalled by gloomy warnings. The crossing was set for the 29th of June; and on the evening of the 28th the sky, which until then had been clear and cloudless, became suddenly overcast, and a most frightful storm burst over Poland. A torrent of rain transformed the ground into liquid mud, in which were bivouacked the poor Italian soldiers.

As to the horses, they fell by hundreds, especially those driven in teams, being for the most part too young to stand the rough service demanded of them, and weakened by insufficient nourishment. By reason of the immense number of horses (one hundred and fifty thousand), which were hastily placed in requisition for the needs of the Grand Army, their recruitment, particularly of those whose fate it was to drag heavy loads, had left much to be desired as regarded quality.

In the course of the marches of concentration, men and beasts had been subjected to frightful torments; but in his letter to the Princess, whose condition of health called for the greatest care for several months yet, Eugene drew a veil over all these sufferings.

The day the Niemen was crossed, he was careful in writing to his wife to make no allusion to the awful tempest which was raging at that moment and devastating everything before it:

NIEMEN, June 29, 1812.

MY DEAR AUGUSTA, — I am writing you from the shores of the Niemen in my tent. The troops are crossing the bridges which I had thrown across the river, and here we are at last in Russia. I am well, and have very few other worries besides those of lack of provisions. Embrace our dear mother for me.

The evening of the 29th and the next day the crossing continued, being rendered very difficult by the storm which prevailed with unabated violence. Wind, hail, rain, and thunder were jumbled together in this tempest; and the bridges thrown across the river were in danger of being carried away.

The frightened troops were almost paralysed. The cavalrymen were obliged to walk beside their horses, guiding them by the bridle, while the infantry pressed close against each other for support.

The waters had risen so high on both shores that the poor soldiers could not find a dry foot of earth, and the horses were dying by thousands.

Panic spread among the Bavarians, and the Italians were worn out by the fatigue of their extraordinary marches. The Prince's energy was powerless to establish discipline; and the laggards, ready to desert their flags, had already commenced to pillage the waggons, which they had been forced to abandon on account of the impracticability of the roads. What a disastrous beginning for a still more disastrous campaign! In his letter of July 4, written from Nowo-Troky, the Prince outlines in very reserved language a feeble sketch of this sombre tableau of a strange war utterly without precedent: —

" Every one believes there will be a battle soon. Three days from now is the anniversary of Wagram; but the Russians are retreating, and are contenting themselves with burning and devastating the country."

Then, as the Empress Josephine had hastened to her daughter-in-law's side to comfort and care for her, he adds these few simple words, which show what a sincere affection existed between these two women who were both so dear to him:

"I need not recommend you to my dèar mother's care: she knows how dearly I love you; she will care for you by her attachment to me and to you."

II.

Eugene finally joined the Emperor at Wilna, where, to his joy, he found four letters from the Princess. He replied to them the sixth of July at eight o'clock in the morning.

" I found your letters of the 16th, 17th, 18th, and 19th of June awaiting me at Wilna. You can imagine what pleasure they gave me. Would you believe it, that on the 1st of July, after a terrible storm, we were obliged to light fires? There is hardly any night here, for at ten o'clock in the evening you can see to read a letter plainly, and before two o'clock in the morning it is daylight. The Emperor asked me all about you yesterday, and I begged him to permit me to give his name to the coming little one if it is a boy. He answered, ' Yes, willingly.' "

The march continued to the front, without any truce, and almost without provisions. It was over most frightful roads.

Eugene, whose natural frankness made it repugnant to him to dissimulate the truth, yet who could not bring himself to distress the Princess with the story of the sufferings the whole army endured, preferred to let her believe he lacked time to write, and made his letters further apart.

It was not until after he had left Wilna three days — that is to say, July 9 — that he wrote from Soleczniky : —

"I could not write to you, my dear Augusta, since leaving Wilna, because for the last three days I have not had a moment's rest. We are running after Bagration's army, and we are having great trouble in joining it. I am well, though all my luggage is behind me, and I only have a portmanteau with me. I think we shall get a rest in a few days, as we have marched all day and every day since leaving Plock."

And quickly as usual the general disappeared to give place to the passionately devoted husband and loving father : —

"I think this letter will reach you near your *accouchement*. It will carry my regrets at being so far away from you, and my hopes for your speedy recovery, and ten big kisses for the little one who shall have come into the world."

The Prince, seeing his splendid troops cut down, so to speak, before his eyes, as well as the entire Grand Army, by illness, fatigue, and desertion, shared Napoleon's feverish haste to reach the enemy and force him into battle.

His particular object was to bring about a meeting with the redoubtable Hetman of the

Cossacks, Platow. Notwithstanding his forced marches, oftentimes extended until midnight, by roads which were almost impracticable, in which he lost a number of horses, and with his exhausted, starving men falling at every step, he did not succeed in reaching him.

After five days of incessant marches, across a devastated and uncultivated country, he finally succeeded in obtaining, at Smorghoni, a stock of bread and beer which had escaped the destruction of the Cossacks, and upon which the unfortunate soldiers threw themselves with avidity.

The following day, July 13, he wrote to his wife — that sweet wife, whose image never left his thoughts in the midst of these cruel vicissitudes — these lines which he strove to render light-hearted : —

SMORGHONI, July 13, 1812, Evening.

I will despatch Fortis the courier to-morrow, my very dear Augusta, and hope he will arrive in time for your *fête ;* he has promised me to be in Milan by August 1. I am sending you but a small remembrance, but it is all I have by me at the present moment. I add the assurance of my eternal love, which you so well merit. Embrace our dear little ones for me. I send you a thousand kisses, which will be very cold when they reach you, though they come from the bottom of my heart. We have been in front of the enemy for

twenty days, and they have not fired twenty balls. As
for myself, I have seen only one Cossack, and he was a
prisoner. It would not surprise me if this campaign
(to be more extraordinary than all the others) should
end without a battle.

Eugene's heart, bleeding for the sufferings of
his soldiers, beat with joy when they were fortunate enough to come across provisions which
the Russians had not had time to destroy. But
this good fortune happened very seldom, and
his corps of the army suffered the most.

On July 24, reaching the Dwina, the light
infantry of the Italian army at last and for the
first time came in sight of the Russians on the
opposite bank. The brave pontoniers dashed
hastily into the water to construct their bridges,
which advanced only too slowly to suit the
anxious army. A ford was discovered; and Eugene, in his impatience, dashed across at the head
of his Bavarian cavalry, reached the other shore,
and galloped on the enemy, who, faithful to their
tactics, disappeared quickly from view.

In the afternoon, when the Emperor crossed
the bridge on horseback, he was greeted with
wild enthusiasm by the Italian soldiers, who then
saw him for the first time. At his appearance

an indescribable frenzy spread among them; and they forgot the fatigues and the hunger undergone, and thought only of the glory to which his genius could not fail to conduct them.

From the camp before the Witepsk, Eugene wrote a short note to the Princess, to announce to her that he had been skirmishing with his corps for four days.

The Prince, who commanded the infantry of the advance-guard, was constantly exposed to great danger. He had made marked efforts to force the Russians into decisive action; but when in the daytime they were seen ranged in battle-array they were nearly always sure to disperse during the night. They had a sanguinary combat at Ostrowno, however, in which the army corps commanded by the Russian general, Osterman, was completely destroyed. Barclay de Tolly manœuvred the Russian rear-guard into a strong position, but they were unable to hold it before the impetuous charge of the Italian Guard and of Murat's cavalry.

The Russians lost, besides ten cannons, four thousand men in these successive combats, three thousand of whom were killed or taken prisoners, — grand results, due for the most part to the ardour which the Viceroy had aroused in his soldiers' hearts.

But these valiant troops were thoroughly exhausted by the fatigue of these ceaseless marches. They were badly in need of sleep, which Napoleon, in the impossibility of bringing the two hostile armies into action, granted them. To give the corps time to be reconstructed and rested, and to rally the numerous stragglers, the Emperor resolved to remain six days in Witepsk.

III.

In the midst of the excessive fatigues of this war, of these marches and battles in a country so far away that the couriers spent twenty-five days on the road between Witepsk and Milan, Eugene never for a moment ceased to be in heart and thought with his little family. At the end of the month then commencing was his wife's fête-day. Could he forget so dear a date? So that his best wishes should arrive by the 28th, he wrote August 3, from his headquarters before Witepsk : —

" To-day is your *fête*, my very dear Augusta, and I try to gladden myself in thinking of the happiness of

those who are near enough to you to wish you joy
personally, and to tell you how much they love you.
I, who am the first among them, without doubt, — I am
not so happy, and my regrets mingle with the joy of
this day."

Then, after modestly mentioning that the
"Emperor was satisfied with his army corps,"
he speaks of the constant difficulty of the question of subsistence, a cause of so much worry to
the commander.

"Our supplies are assured for eight days, and will be,
I hope, for fifteen. How grand this will be!"

Foreseeing the painful thoughts of the Princess,
he cries out, as he ends his letter: —

"Adieu, my cherished wife! when you look at the
maps and see how far away we are from each other, it
must make you tremble; but be of good cheer, and
keep a brave heart."

In the mean time the Grand Army under
Napoleon was approaching Smolensk. The day
after the victory of Krasnoi, which was won
on Napoleon's birthday, they were in marching
order.

What a difference there was between this
Russian 15th of August and the other *fêtes*
celebrated with such pomp and joy! Neverthe-

less, in spite of the sinister omens of this war, so little like all that had gone before, in which, instead of pursuing an unapproachable enemy, the army passed from success to triumphs, the Emperor's *fête* must not pass unnoticed.

From daybreak the deepening roar of the cannon, so sweet to the ears of a soldier, was heard in honour of the still unconquered Napoleon! All day noisy salutes of artillery resounded joyously on the distant shores of the Dnieper. Napoleon was deeply touched by this fresh proof of the enthusiasm of his army, — an army, alas! already diminished one-half by the constant attacks of an evil against which the great general had never before been obliged to struggle, — desertion!

The Emperor's headquarters were naturally the centre of communication with the Empire. It was from his lips that Eugene learned with emotion the expected news very dear to his heart: the birth of a new child, who had been six weeks in the world before her father could be informed.

With what haste the latter wrote to the Princess! —

IN CAMP, August 17, 1812, Midday.

The Emperor has just announced to me, my dear Augusta, your happy *accouchement* of a little girl on

July 3. He received the tidings by telegraph from Milan to Paris, and he imparted this good news to me this morning. I thank Heaven with all my heart! I have marched all night. I preceded the troops in order to join the Emperor here and congratulate him on his *fête.* Take great care of yourself."

Two days later, amid the roar of cannon, Eugene resumed his familiar chat, — for these letters are really less of a correspondence than a familiar and almost uninterrupted chat. From the camp at Smolensk, he writes to his wife, August 19, 1812: —

MY DEAR AUGUSTA, — I have not been able to write to you for three days, as we have been in the presence of the enemy all of the time. The Emperor had decided to attack the city of Smolensk; and it was captured with much loss of life on the part of the enemy. My corps of the army was not actively engaged. Yesterday we saw the whole Russian army ranged in battle. We were to have opened fire on them this morning, but the army disappeared during the night, leaving only a rear-guard in sight. I can hear the cannons roar as I write you. My troops have just crossed the river.

Eugene, as can be seen, passes over in silence all that could frighten the Princess too much in the particularly horrible aspects of this campaign. For instance, when he writes of the capture of

Smolensk, he takes good care not to speak of
the incendiaries of the Russians, who, fully understanding the uselessness of all resistance,
and wishing, according to their infernal tactics,
to spread ruin in the path of the French army,
set fire to the city during the night. Smolensk
in flames seen from the French camp was so
frightfully grand in its aspect that Napoleon, in
his bulletin, compares it to "an eruption of
Vesuvius on a beautiful summer's night"!

Following Eugene's example, I will also gloss
over the horrors of this barbarous war, and keep
myself as much as possible within the delicate
frame of these charming letters, which it is difficult to conceive of as being written in the midst
of this campaign.

What Eugene could not hide from the Princess, notwithstanding the fears with which this
fact could not help inspiring her on the subject
of the interminable length of his absence, was
the persistence with which the Russians always
avoided a battle.

" We have surrounded this city for the last three days;
but the Emperor has ordered all his generals to the
front. At nightfall, the enemy was seen to be occupying a splendid position, but they disappeared during

the night. In consequence, there was no appearance
of a battle, though we were all prepared for it. This
delay enrages me. The days are intensely hot, and the
nights equally cold. They tell us the cold weather will
be upon us in less than a month. Adieu.

"Your faithful husband and lifelong friend."

Four days later he writes from Dorogoboge:

"Since I left Smolensk, we have been constantly on
the march, and we have reached Dorogoboge quickly,
where the enemy is said to be ready for battle, awaiting
us. Not one word of truth in the rumour, as I learned
when our troops arrived, at midday."

And he adds, using a little indirect flattery
to the Princess, by praising her countrymen, —

"I think I told you that the Bavarian troops had
quite an affair near Polozk. They covered themselves
with glory."

Two days later, Eugene is unwillingly obliged
to admit to his wife that nearly all his generals
and aides-de-camp are ill, and unfit for active
service; but he only refers lightly to this painful
subject, and dwells, on the contrary, on an interview he had had with Napoleon, and in which
the latter dwelt lovingly on the dear absentees.

August 27, 1812, Evening.

Yesterday my corps of the army marched towards
Dorogoboge, where the Emperor is at present. I went

to see him; he was very kind to me, and asked after you most anxiously. He knows nothing gives me more pleasure than that. Adieu, my dear Augusta. In a few days I may write to you from Moscow.

At length the moment so ardently longed for approached. The great battle was imminent. The Russians, notwithstanding their intention to destroy the French army by fatigue, by cold, and by famine, rather than by bullets, were obliged to make at least a semblance of defending the Holy City, Moscow.

General Kutusoff, an astute old man who had just been placed at the head of the Russian army, excelled in this mode of warfare, so approved of by public opinion; but the military element innate in every soldier excited feelings of shame at the idea of never facing the enemy. Kutusoff experienced great difficulties in satisfying the general wish, which agreed so well with his particular views, without running counter to the ideas of the Russian fanatics who were so anxious to fight.

This discontent had assumed such proportions that when rumour gave out that they were not going to defend the Holy City, Kutusoff could see no alternative but to declare his intention of barring the road to Moscow against the French army.

On the other side, the march upon Moscow had not been decided at the French headquarters without a great deal of discussion. Napoleon, who had been detained at Ghat by the bad condition of the roads, reduced to bogs by the continuous rains, found himself solicited by Berthier, Ney, Murat, and nearly all the marshals not to continue this foolhardy march, which threatened to annihilate what remained of the Grand Army. They asked him to retrace his steps and spend the winter in Poland, and from there in the spring march upon St. Petersburg with three hundred thousand rested men.

For one moment Napoleon was on the point of yielding to these prayers, the weight of which he understood only too well; but having until then astonished the world by the exploits of the overwhelming grandeurs of his operations, he feared that drawing back at this period would throw a shadow over his military prestige, and that his power, which rested with him entirely, would be overthrown.

Fine weather setting in just at this juncture, and the roads in this vicinity becoming once more practicable, Napoleon ceased to hesitate. He ordered the Grand Army forward, crying out, "The die is cast; we must meet the Russians!"

"On the eve of this celebrated battle," as Constant tells us, "there arrived from Paris to Napoleon the portrait of the King of Rome. This loving attention, which had come as a diversion to him in the midst of his grave anxieties, caused him great happiness. He held the portrait on his knee for a long time, gazing at it in ecstasy, and said 'it was the most agreeable surprise which had ever been given him.' He repeated several times in a low voice, 'My dear Louise! this is a loving attention!' The Emperor's face was overspread with an expression of intense happiness difficult to describe. His first emotions were calm and tinged with melancholy; 'The dear child!' this was all he said."

But his paternal love and pride beamed forth as the officers and even the men of the Old Guard came, according to his orders, to gaze upon the features of the King of Rome. The portrait was exposed before the Emperor's tent. Nothing could be more touching and at the same time more majestic than the spectacle of these old

soldiers, uncovering respectfully before the picture in which they searched for some resemblance
to Napoleon. The Emperor at that moment was
filled with the excessive joy of a father, who knew
that after him his son had no better friends than
the old companions of his fatigues and glory.

IV.

Eugene's *rôle* on this famous day of Moscow
was one of the most important, and one which
showed the absolute confidence Napoleon had in
his military talents.

The Russians had thrown up some very strong
earthworks. It was the strongest of these which
the Prince received orders to attack and capture
at any price.

Eugene made his first move, at six o'clock in
the morning, by a vigorous attack on the village
of Borodino, a very important position, which he
captured and kept all day. Eugene sent Mo-
rand's brave division to take possession of the
main fort, which, after a desperate struggle against
superior numbers, found itself on the point of
being driven back from the summit of the works.
Just at this critical moment the Prince arrived

on the scene at the head of his other troops, re-established confidence, and victoriously planted the French flag on the plateau under the death-dealing fire of the enemy. As far back as we may go in history, no other battle cost what the battle of Moscow did in renowned generals and officers with brilliant futures.

How the poor Vice-Queen would have trembled could she have seen death at every moment of this murderous struggle pass so close to her beloved husband!

The battle was to all appearances won. Suddenly the left flank of the French army, which the Russians were endeavouring to overthrow, recoiled under an attack and were put to flight. Eugene perceived the position at a glance, saw the imminent peril, dashed towards Borodino under a shower of balls, finding his regiments drawn up in squares to repulse the massed charges of the innumerable Russian cavalry, and soon led the tricolour back to victory.

The principal fort in the mean time having been retaken by the Russians, Napoleon ordered Eugene to capture this position from the enemy, it being the last point of resistance remaining to them. He placed himself at the head of one

Marie Anne Elise Bonaparte, Grand Duchess of Tuscany.

of the picked regiments, the Ninth of the Line, spoke a few energetic words which made a lion of every French soldier, bounded to the summit of the redoubt amid a rain of bullets, captured the earthwork, and held it victoriously. This manœuvre definitely assured the victory to the French army.

Eugene was one of the few generals who passed through the infernal fire, which lasted from daybreak until sunset, unwounded and safely. Constant gives us some idea of the awful carnage of this battle, whose killed numbered ninety thousand men in both camps : —

"The Emperor," he says, "haunted the battle-field. It was a horrible sight, nearly all the dead bodies being covered with wounds, which proved with what fury they had fought. It had commenced to rain; a high wind was blowing. The wounded, who had not yet been carried away in ambulances, half raised themselves from the ground to attract attention and not be overlooked. There were some among them who cried out as Napoleon passed, in spite of their sufferings and exhaustion, ' Long live the Emperor!' Those of our soldiers who had been struck by Russian balls, displayed wounds as large as big holes, for their balls were much bigger than ours. We saw a standard-bearer enveloped in his flag as in a shroud. He seemed to give signs of life, but expired as they lifted him from the ground."

In terms of most admirable simplicity the Prince announces to his Vice-Queen this most sanguinary of victories, qualifying by the words "devoir accompli" the heroic part he had taken :

ON THE BATTLE-FIELD, September 8, 8 A. M.

I have only time to write you two words, my very dear Augusta, to tell you that I am very well. We fought a grand battle yesterday, hotly contested and redounding greatly to the Emperor's glory. I commanded the left wing, and we did our duty! Picture my happiness if you can! Yesterday before midnight I was sleeping, bivouacked with the soldiers. Fortis awoke me, bringing me your dear letter and charming present. . . . Adieu. Rest tranquil. We are marching on Moscow, and after so cruel a battle every one needs repose.

The present so appreciated by Eugene was a miniature portrait of his three children, a veritable "group of angels." He writes thus to Darnay : —

"You must know by this time, my dear Darnay, of our great battle. Imagine a more sanguinary and terrible affray than Wagram, at which you assisted. Those who came out safe and sound can thank Heaven! Fortis, the courier, reached here precisely at midnight after the great battle. He did well not to come until afterwards. The portrait of my little family touched me greatly."

The day after this dearly bought victory, the Grand Army set out on its march on Moscow. The idea of at last occupying a great city, where every one hoped to find abundance of food and rest, had made all hearts light and gay.

Here are a few lines from Eugene, who had caught the contagion of the light-heartedness of the sorely tried army : —

IN A CHÂTEAU, SIX LEAGUES AND A HALF FROM MOSCOW,
September 13, 1812.

MY DEAR AUGUSTA, —You can see by the date of my letter that we are very near Moscow; and if we do not enter to-morrow, our entrance cannot be long delayed. It has been rumoured that the Russians will fight us again before Moscow; but I cannot believe it after the lesson they have received, and the panic which reigns among them, and the disordered condition of their army. It is commencing to be very cold here; and we indeed need to reach a great city to provide ourselves with the necessaries we so sadly need. Goodnight; I am going to take supper now and go to bed. It is eight o'clock, and I have been on horseback all day facing Messieurs les Cosaques.

V.

On September 14, the French army, from the summit of the surrounding hills, at last saw lying before them Moscow's gilded domes. What pride

filled the hearts of these soldiers who, following
the footsteps of the grand conqueror, had tri-
umphantly entered every European capital!
Moscow, the Holy City of the Russian Empire,
had alone been sacred from them; and there she
lay at their mercy at the present moment, colossal,
magnificent, with her vast palaces and superb
churches, dominated by the Kremlin, ancient for-
tress and palace of the Czar!

On September 15, Napoleon, deeply affected
at seeing Moscow at his mercy, the last favour
of a fortune up to that moment fabulous, made
his entry into the city, — a city which had been
vibrating with life the day before, but which was
like a city of the dead to-day!

The Russian Governor, Count Rostopchin, a
fanatical patriot, had, in fact, ordered nearly all
the population to vacate the city. In his hatred
of the conqueror, and in order to deprive him of
the benefits of his conquest, he conceived the
awful revenge of delivering Moscow to the flames.
Before leaving the city he had opened the doors
of the prison and put incendiary torches into the
hands of the criminals. In his revengeful precautions he had given the barbarous order to
carry away all the pumps, with the fiendish idea

of rendering the enemy powerless to extinguish the conflagration.

In the mean time, the Emperor, in the flush of his triumph, had installed himself in the Kremlin. How did he learn of this disaster which was to suddenly change his whole destiny? We will give Constant's version of it: —

"It was two o'clock in the morning when the news was announced to the Emperor that the city was on fire. Frenchmen living in the country and an officer of the Russian police confirmed the news and entered into details too precise in their nature to leave any doubt in the Emperor's mind as to the truth of their assertion. However, he still persisted in not believing it.

"'But it is not possible! Can you believe such a thing, Constant? Go and see if it is true.'

"Then he threw himself back on his bed, trying to get a little rest. In a few moments he called me again to ask the same questions. . . .

"The Emperor passed the night in violent agitation. When day broke, he knew the worst. . . .

"Soon the most incredible reports commenced to pour in. Russians had been caught feeding the flames and throwing inflammable materials into the portions of the houses still standing intact. The Russians who were taking no active part in the incendiary work stood with crossed arms, contemplating the disaster with an impassibility of which you could conceive no idea. . . .

"The Russian soldiers and police had been seen stir-

ring up the flames with their iron lances.   Shells placed
in the stoves of several houses had burst and wounded
many of our soldiers.   In the streets filthy, hideous
women and drunken men ran to the burning houses,
and, snatching burning fagots, were about to carry them
elsewhere to spread the conflagration.   Our soldiers
were obliged many times to beat them out of their
hands with their swords. . . .

" Napoleon, who had gone out to satisfy himself as to
the true condition of affairs, had his gray coat burned
in several places, and his hair singed.   A moment later
we were walking over firebrands."

The fire spread so rapidly that even the distant
Kremlin, where Napoleon lodged, was at one time
in danger.   Great sparks driven by the high
winds fell in the large park where the ammunition was stored, and threatened to blow up the
Kremlin with its illustrious inmate and the Imperial Guard.   In consequence of this fierce conflagration, the Emperor and his army were forced
to evacuate Moscow for a few days.

Eugene, with his ever-present thought not to
frighten the Princess, contents himself with saying
on the subject of this irreparable catastrophe:

Moscow, September 15, 1812.

MY DEAR AUGUSTA, — I write to you from the sub-
urbs of Moscow, where I am quartered with my corps
of the army.   The Russians evacuated the city yesterday,

but, before going, set fire to it in twenty different places, especially in the merchants' quarters, where all the stores are located, consequently all the provisions. Nothing could have been more barbarous. The army will get a good rest, I hope; and this rest will be a good time to repair our luggage and utensils. The cold is very severe, and will be worse before another month comes around.

This city is grand. It contains magnificent palaces side by side with wretched huts. On the whole, though, it is a beautiful city; but as the nobility and rich have fled, there remains only the populace.

Two days later, while the great fire continued its ravages, — a fire which lasted four days and destroyed four-fifths of Moscow, — he writes again:

MOSCOW, September 17, 1812, Evening.

MY DEAR AUGUSTA, —Allari, the courier, will hand you this letter. He will give you the details of the grand battle, which he witnessed from afar. He can also tell you how far the Russians carried their barbarism. They set fire to the immense city of Moscow, and you can conceive no idea of the horrible spectacle we have had before our eyes for the last three days. The city is still burning. My health continues good, and would be better if I only had the hope of seeing you soon to cheer me up.

The courier being delayed the next day, Eugene, on second thought, preferring that the Princess should learn all the details of the catastrophe,

which entirely changed the situation, traced the
following touching picture: —

Moscow, September 18, 1812, Evening.

I could not send Allari off yesterday, as I had thought
to, as I was obliged to be with the Emperor all day,
my very dear Augusta. I cannot get him off before
to-morrow at daybreak; and he will be all of twenty-
eight or thirty days on the road. The city is almost
entirely reduced to ashes, and it was one of the handsomest in Europe. It contains some magnificent palaces,
in a great number of which the barbaric gorgeousness of
the Russian taste was displayed in all its lavishness. In
setting fire to this city, they ruined three hundred thousand inhabitants and six hundred of the most powerful
nobles in Russia, for the sake of depriving us of some
provisions in flour, wine, clothes, and shoes. We have
succeeded in arresting about thirty of these miserable
bandits just in time to prevent them from starting fresh
fires. Many were massacred on the spot by our furious
soldiers. Enough remained for us to judge of them,
and among them is an officer wearing a Russian decoration. All these wretches have confessed that they
were paid to do this, and that they only acted under
the Governor of Moscow's orders. You cannot imagine
anything to equal the horrible spectacle we have had
under our eyes during this fire. There still remain
eighty or one hundred thousand inhabitants in the city.
They are at present without food, without clothing, without a shelter for their heads, at the approach of a season
which is severe indeed. It is horrible to contemplate.

It can easily be imagined that in the days following these scenes of desolation before Moscow in ashes, life was deplorably sad for the army. While awaiting an order to march forward, the officers and soldiers amused themselves as they could:

IN CAMP NEAR MOSCOW, September 21, 1812.

A terrible storm has been raging since day before yesterday, my very dear Augusta. It only ceased raining this morning, and we were glad indeed to see signs of approaching clear weather. I am holding myself in readiness for marching orders. There is a question of sending some troops forward toward St. Petersburg, and it will probably be my corps of the army. The location of winter-quarters is being discussed; and it is almost certain there will be no more fighting this year. It is even thought the Russians will consent to peace when they see we are determined to maintain our footing in the country.

I imagine that you follow all our movements on the map, and I am sure you can obtain a good one of Russia. I passed yesterday evening with the Emperor. We play *vingt-et-un* to while away the time. I foresee we are going to find the evenings very long: there is not the slightest distraction for us, not even billiards. Adieu, my dear Augusta; without distractions, as with all the amusements in the world at my disposal, I desire you just as ardently, and the companionship of my little ones.

On September 24, when three months must still elapse before the New Year, Eugene sent some presents to Milan, — a delicate attention most natural on the part of a husband filled with tender solicitude as was Eugene, who, at this early date, was oppressed with uncertainties for the future.

Moscow, September 24, 1812, Evening.

As I cannot tell how much longer our communications will be open, I take advantage of the departure of the courier to send you these New Year's gifts. The furs are the handsomest I could buy in all this disorder. It is a long time ahead for New Year's gifts; but it is still possible that everything is over for the present, and in that case I shall go to you myself. I will endeavour to find something for the little ones, but this is very difficult: they are all bears here.

The following letter was positive proof of these precautions, and shows that his haste to profit by the departure of a courier was foresight on his part:

Moscow, September 26, 1812.

MY VERY DEAR AUGUSTA, —I wrote to you twice the day before yesterday, — by the express in the morning, the courier in the evening; but the latter has been unable to set out, on account of a party of Cossacks who are harassing our rear. I am afraid that some of my letters will serve as amusement for them instead of tranquillising you.

To calm his wife is the constant thought of the Prince, who, after each letter received from her, never failed to despatch a courier, or, if need be, an officer, with a letter.

On September 27 snow commenced to fall, an early herald of the rigours of this winter, which was destined to annihilate this hitherto victorious French army. As though he wished, by evoking agreeable remembrances, to take his thoughts from the sad reality which surrounded him, Eugene worried over the least and most minute details of the life the Princess led so far away from him.

Moscow, September 28, 1812.

The courier has at last set out with the furs and a small provision of tea. He will arrive, I hope, in time for the first of your evenings, when this tea will replace the ices. Here we shall have more ice than tea, and every one is wrapping himself up in consequence. For my part, I shall be in furs from head to foot. It snowed a little yesterday. To-day the air is dry and cold. This is better than the heavy rains we have been having. I received your letters of the 4th, 5th, and 6th of September, and am glad to learn that you are feeling well. I share the sorrow you express at my mother's departure. You will feel very lonely and sad now that she has left you. I suppose you are comfortably established at Monza. Did you find it much improved? Do the hares still eat the young trees? Are there many pheasants? Did you see about the villa? These few little details it would please me greatly to know about.

The army having ceased to march and fight, Eugene was only too happy to be able by this short respite to take up the sweet habit of chatting each day, and oftener twice than once, with his wife. The courier carrying the preceding letter had not accomplished the first day of his journey when Eugene wrote again, while under the influence of the intense pleasure he had felt upon receiving the little souvenirs sent by the Vice-Queen and the Empress Josephine.

Moscow, September 29, 1812.

You can picture my joy on receiving such good news of my little family. I thank you a thousand times for the watch-chain. Every one at the Emperor's head-quarters complimented me on it this evening. I shall attach the key and seal sent by the Empress. I had a few of my generals and marshals to dinner to-day ; and the habitual dessert of showing the portraits of the five beings dearest to my heart passed off with great *éclat*.

VI.

Napoleon, though victorious, recognised the urgent desire felt by the army, exhausted by long marches rather than by battles, for a treaty of

peace before the season of intense cold, and before he could decide upon his winter headquarters. He made several overtures to Alexander
on the subject, but his advances were fruitless.
What was he to do? Napoleon had mapped
out a most brilliant manœuvre, — an oblique
march towards the north, which would have
brought him close to the magazines of Poland,
and at the same time made possible a siege of St.
Petersburg. But his marshals declared unanimously that the army was not in a condition to
risk long tramps over unknown routes.

The question of wintering in Moscow was
mooted. Daru, Secretary of State, who had accompanied Napoleon as Adjutant-General of the
army, and was consequently the best judge of
the matter, had recommended this plan, judging
it easier to feed the army at Moscow, where there
was a stock of provisions sufficient for several
months, than to lead it to Poland across icy
roads. The idea of passing the winter among the
ashes of Moscow, which prevailed for a moment,
gave rise doubtless to the unexpected demand
made by Napoleon to Eugene to import some
Italian singers to enliven the monotony of their
sad winter residence.

Moscow, October 1, 1812.

The question of remaining here for the winter is being discussed, but every one hopes the enemy will think twice before dooming us to remain here, instead of making terms of peace; but all and each of us try to bear our part bravely, and you know how much it will cost me to be still further away from you and my little ones. The Emperor is thinking of having some actors sent from Paris and some singers from Milan; and yet, in spite of all this, you may imagine we shall pass our winter coldly and sadly.

Reading over the following letter, which makes an allusion to the project of having actors and singers sent to Moscow, one asks oneself if it were not a pretence destined to inspire the enemy with more peaceful reflections: —

Moscow, October 9, 1812.

It is to be hoped that matters will arrange themselves soon for the winter. The more preparations we make for remaining here, the more urgent the Russians will be to see us evacuate one way or another. Do not get frightened when you hear we intend sending for actors; that we shall give dramas, etc. All this will only tend to satisfy the Russians that we are not going to leave them as soon as they thought we should, and they will act more quickly. The weather has been very fine for the past few days. The sick men are recovering, and we are now laying in a stock of provisions for the winter, and clothing and furs. We are expecting

windmills from France, with which to grind our corn.
We shall have made, by our vanquished difficulties and
the rapidity of our marches, the most astonishing campaign and the shortest we have ever experienced up to
the present time.

In spite of the mournful sadness of his present
existence, Eugene, true French soldier as he was,
did not lose his sense of humour. He joked as
he depicted the Russian cold: —

Moscow, October 18, 1812.

It seems we are not to leave either to-day or to-
morrow. There is some parley at headquarters, but I
think of little consequence. I think you had better
remain at Monza until the middle of November, especially if the fine weather continues. Do not expect to
see us return as we set out, for they tell me the noses
and ears of strangers freeze very easily in winter here.
We shall all be very homely if they leave us here.

A sharp and sudden frost forced Napoleon to
put an end to his indecision. On October 19,
the army left the Holy City; and under a clear
sky Eugene and his companions saw for the last
time the few gilded domes which the fire fiends
had spared. The never-to-be-forgotten retreat
from Russia had commenced.

CHAPTER VII.

Retreat from Russia. — Misery and Sanguinary Combats. —
Smolensk. — The Beresina. — The Emperor leaves the Army.
— The Twenty-ninth Bulletin. — Last Proofs. — Defections.
— Adieux to the Cossacks.

I.

LEAVING Moscow, Napoleon imagined he
was pursuing the Russians, momentarily at
least, and not entering upon the most disastrous
of retreats. The first encounter took place at
Malo-Jaroslawetz, where the Russians endeavoured to bar his passage.

Malo-Jaroslawetz is a village situated on a hill.
The French were obliged to cross the Lougéa,
— a river running at the foot of this village, —
and to climb the hill under a murderous fire, to
wrench this important position from the Russians. The enemy was not only in a position to
bar the way, but also to throw the French back
into the Lougéa. General Delzous, who, under
Eugene's orders, had gained the heights, and
taken the village at the point of the bayonet,

fell, mortally wounded. His brother, who had stood beside him, and who had tried to save his body from the enemy, was also killed.

The French were on the point of being repulsed, when Eugene dashed forward, and under the terrible artillery fire of the Russians, climbed the hill, strewn with the dead and dying. Six times the village was taken and retaken by furious charges in the midst of the flames of the neighbouring houses, which enveloped the combatants; but nothing could make this intrepid Prince, ready to die or to sacrifice his last man rather than leave the Russians master of a position upon which depended the welfare of the army, abandon his enterprise. He called the Pino Division and the Royal Italian Guard to his assistance; and after a furious hand-to-hand struggle, he succeeded in capturing Malo-Jaroslawetz for the seventh time, and held it victoriously in the midst of the smoking ruins.

He announced this grand feat of arms in the following simple words to the Princess:—

MALO-JAROSLAWETZ, October 25, 1812.

I have only time to write a few words, my dear Augusta. I am very well. Yesterday was a grand day for my corps of the army. We fought from morning until night with eight divisions of the enemy ; but I kept my position. French and Italians covered themselves with glory.

The *Journal de l'Empire* describes in a much more detailed manner the heroic part taken by Eugene in this sanguinary battle : —

" The latest news from the Emperor is under date of November 3d. His Majesty is in the best of health. The weather continues fine, and the army are moving forward in the most perfect order since the vigorous lesson the enemy received at Malo-Jaroslawetz.

" This brilliant affair reflects the greatest honour on the corps under command of the Viceroy of Italy. In this engagement the Prince proved himself the worthy pupil of the great captain under whom he learned the art of war ; and he displayed in his tactics the bravery of a young warrior, joined to the experience of an old general. The Russians, superior in number, returned ten times to the charge, and ten times were they repulsed from the battle-field, strewing it with their dead and wounded. The Prince, rallying his soldiers by his presence, planned his attacks calmly, and executed them vigorously. When, after the enemy's retreat, His Imperial Highness passed the division in review, the troops greeted him with the wildest enthusiasm, and unanimous acclamations were heard all along the line."

In writing the details of this battle for the Emperor, Eugene, with his usual modesty, generously forgot himself, to cover the generals and officers who had fought under him with the warmest praises.

His description written for the Emperor gives several very interesting details of the different phases of this furious fight: —

"Three times the Russians succeeded in driving us back to the river, and three times our troops rallied before the bridge, and, aided by the reserves in the advance-guard, dashed up the hill in a mad, impetuous charge on the first Russian batteries, shouting, 'Vive l'Empereur!' The position of their army was protected by an embankment whose summit was fortified by three redoubts, and over which fresh columns of attacking men climbed every minute. Their generals led them to the attack against us eight times, but the French and Italian troops rivalled them in intrepidity. We repulsed all their attacks at the bayonet-point, and the Russians left the ground covered with their dead.

"I must draw Your Majesty's attention to the fact that all the regiments of my corps of the army covered themselves with glory. French and Italian vied with each other in giving testimony to Your Majesty of their devotion and love."

Eugene, after giving the names of several of the generals and colonels, concluded by this touching appeal to Napoleon in favour of the family of General Delzous: —

"The Fourth Army Corps are deeply grieved over General Delzous's death. To tell Your Majesty that he leaves a wife, four children, and twelve brothers without means of any kind, is to assure their comfort for the future."

I have dwelt at length on this battle, which was so glorious for Eugene, for the reason that, with twenty thousand men under his command, he battled against and overcame an opposing force of eighty thousand, and has handed down to history one of the finest feats of arms in the astonishing campaigns which Napoleon's military genius offers to the admiration of posterity!

After such a terrible struggle, and a whole day spent on horseback, in the midst of the fatigues and constant anxiety of the hasty march which followed, the loving, thoughtful husband found time to write and reassure the fearful wife so far away from him, and trembling for his life. If he must renounce the hope, which until then had sustained him, of a speedy return home, he rejoiced that his army was to take up its winter-quarters and find a shelter against the intense cold which was making itself already felt: —

Tunechewo, October 26, 1812.

I repeat to you again that I am feeling well, and that the engagement just fought reflected glory on my corps and on myself. We have been marching since midday. It seems we are drawing near our winter-quarters. We must go as far as Siberia to pursue these cursed Russians. You and I must give up the hope of being together as soon as we anticipated; but when we do meet, it is to be hoped that we shall never be separated again. Your letters of the 28th, 29th, and 30th of September have not reached me. It is to be hoped those dear Cossacks are not enjoying them. Adieu. I did not get much sleep last night, and I have been on horseback all day.

In the letter which follows, he speaks for the first time of the intense sufferings caused by the cold, and gives a glimpse of the difficulties of the army's situation, but with what proud confidence in the invincibility of the French arms!

IN CAMP AT MOJAÏSK, October 29, 1812.

I am writing to you, dear Augusta, from the same little château where I was lodged after the battle of Moscow. To all appearances we are drawing near Smolensk, — first, to find rest ; second, to find provisions for the winter. We are commencing to suffer from the cold. It freezes very hard at night, but the weather is very fortunate for us, for the mud does not bother us now that the ground is frozen over. It is rumoured that the enemy has become more courageous since we left Moscow, and that it is his intention to cut off our route to Smolensk. If this happens, we shall get even with him for the loss of two or three of our couriers, and the enemy will be exterminated.

II.

The Russians, though avoiding a great battle, pursued the French army with unremitting assiduity, enveloping it with a cloud of Cossacks, and trying to cut off the straggling columns in order to destroy them. At Tsaréwo-Zaïmitché the Viceroy's corps, crossing over a narrow, dangerous gorge, suddenly found themselves under the fire of a formidable body of Russian artillery aided by many Cossacks. To crown their misfortune, a bridge which was indispensable for the passage of the troops had broken down under the enormous weight of horses and luggage. The peril was extreme. Eugene, putting a brave face on the matter, and exercising his military talent, opened a way through the enemy's ranks; although he had passed the entire night on horseback, he never thought of taking a moment's repose until the last of his men were out of danger.

His march was retarded by thousands of laggards and a number of helpless wounded. On reaching Wiazma, he again found his route barred by a strong force of the enemy's cavalry, and it was only after a rough battle that he was enabled to pierce this living wall. These continuous and hopeless struggles he called *bonnes occupations.*

SEMLOWO, November 4, 1812, 5 P. M.

I do not know how many days have elapsed since I wrote to you, my very dear Augusta. It has been impossible for me to write to you before. Since my engagement at Malo-Jaroslawetz, I have constantly been engaged with *bonnes occupations.* I wrote to you from a little château near Mojaïsk that we were marching forward to find a suitable place for a winter-encampment, and one more accessible to provisions for the army. Since that time, the enemy has amused himself by stinging our rear-guard; and every day we have been attacked by some of their numerous cavalry. At last they opened fire on Marshal Davout yesterday, who was in charge of the rear-guard, and at the same time attacked my flank. For an instant one of my divisions was cut off from me; but Marshal Davout repulsed them, and together we continued our march on Wiazma. Our two corps were separated from the rest of the troops, and the whole of the enemy's army seemed upon us. We executed some fine retrograde movements. Hunger and fatigue bothered us a little; but I think when we reach Smolensk, we shall find more abundance. We need only a few more days of patience to have plenty around us. Adieu, my very dear friend. I leave you now to throw myself on a bearskin and sleep, and God knows I need the latter.

The retreat continued over this desolate route, —a mute witness of the opening battles, when hope in the glory and faith in the future filled their hearts. What a striking contrast! The army once more looked upon the bloody theatres of its vain successes, still covered with the un-buried dead, twisted guns, and demolished gun-carriages. Now they were marching forward, shivering, hungry, and despairing, in a march which already commenced to take upon itself the ugly aspect of a retreat.

Eugene was careful not to write all the details of this sombre picture to his wife, but he dwelt upon little personal discomforts which he thought would bring a smile to her lips rather than afflict her soul, as he knew the avowal of the too lamentable truth would.

He spoke of his privations and perils with a smiling stoicism worthy of the heroic legend which has grown up around those terrible events.

BOLDIN, November 6, 1812, 8 A. M.

. . . The Emperor was very well satisfied with my corps of the army in the last engagement. The enemy has not annoyed us these past few days, and I think we are at the end of our campaign for the present. We have suffered some privations for several days. We are marching over the route the army followed on its march to Moscow, and it is in just such strange circumstances men are tried; it is a good school.

Adieu, my dear Augusta. My health is good. Yesterday I made a toilette of which I stood badly in need. It was — would you believe it? — ten days since I had been shaved. I looked like a Capuchin. . . .

Three days later, Eugene's corps underwent one of those disasters with which the history of this memorable retreat is sown. To enable the army to cross the Wop, swollen and turbulent, filled with great cakes of ice, the Prince had sent his pontoon-builders ahead. Before the bridge was finished, the cattle, crowded forward by the women and children who burdened the army, but whom for humanity's sake it was a duty to protect, precipitated themselves in the darkness over the arches of the unfinished bridge; and the head of this sad column was pitilessly submerged in the swift, angry waters, which closed over them, cutting off a supply of provisions in a manner appalling in its awfulness. The cries of the victims frightened the crowd behind, who rushed ahead in wild confusion. The infantry and cavalry were obliged to cross the Wop on foot, at the price of great sufferings.

The cannons blocked up the ford, rendering it impassable. Added to these horrors, the Cossacks on an opposite hill fired into the crowd of struggling human beings and dumb beasts, from the midst of whom arose cries of despair and women's heart-rending sobs. The Prince crossed the Wop at the head of his troops, dispersed the Cossacks, and worked until nightfall trying to save these unhappy creatures, finally succeeding in placing them in safety on the opposite bank. But the greater part of the luggage, seven or eight pieces of cannon, — that is to say, nearly all of the Viceroy's artillery, — remained buried in the river and had to be abandoned to the enemy.

Eugene in this disaster worked with a superhuman energy without a thought of himself. For the first time he was obliged to admit that he suffered. But if his bodily strength was limited, his brave heart remained the same; his constancy and ardour were incapable of discouragement or weakness. These few following lines are a striking proof of what I have just said : —

DUCHOWSCHTSCHINA, November 11, 1812.

I hasten to give you some news of myself, my dear Augusta. This I have been unable to do for the past four days. My health is fairly good. I say fairly, for I am suffering with one of my limbs, which is very much swollen. I think this is due to fatigue. I have been very much inconvenienced these last few days, for the weather and the season are so bad that to continue my march I have been obliged to abandon part of my artillery and nearly all my luggage. We are greatly in need of rest, and I hope it will not be denied us long. Our misfortunes are great; but when one's courage remains, that is the essential point!

The troops having rested on the 11th and 12th, the advance-guard began its march on Smolensk. To light up the route for the army, they set fire to the miserable wooden huts which lined the wayside, and which had been deserted by their inhabitants. This doleful light indicated the right road to the corps, which followed in their footsteps. The cold was becoming intense. It was decided that it was impossible to take the women any further, these latter having followed the army since leaving Moscow.

Napoleon, on setting out from Smolensk, had committed one of the rare errors of his military career. Persuaded that the Russians would not dare to make any serious attack upon him, he had, instead of keeping the army together, ordered the departure of the different corps on different days. If the Russians did not dare molest Napoleon, surrounded as he was by his Old Guard, they did not experience the same fear with regard to his lieutenants. After allow-ing the Emperor to pass, they barred Eugene's passage at Krasnoï.

Just before reaching Krasnoï is a very steep ravine. Eugene, who had no suspicion of the Russians' intentions, reached the ravine without any warning, to find it bristling with cannon and filled with the enemy's infantry. He had only six thousand men with him, — all that remained to him of the superb army of eighty thousand men, with which he had entered Russia.

With one quick glance, the young general had taken in the situation. He must cut his way, sword in hand, through this compact mass.

Without losing an instant, he ordered Broussier's heroic division to charge at the bayonet's point on the enemy's batteries. The three thousand brave fellows dashed forward only to meet with so murderous a fire that in less than an hour two thousand men lay dead and wounded on the frozen earth. The rest retired without disturbing the enemy's position, bringing back to the Viceroy proofs that it was impossible to overthrow that frightful living wall.

The Russian General Kutusoff, whose entire army stood ready to repulse the four thousand men remaining to the brilliant Italian army, sent an officer to Eugene, requesting him to give himself up.

" Say to your general," replied the Prince, proudly, " that it is better for him to prepare for battle, and not to send for prisoners."

It was near nightfall; and the Russians, judging it useless longer to sacrifice men and ammunition, and thinking that in the morning these intractable Frenchmen would fall an easy prey, ceased hostilities. In this critical circumstance, Josephine's son showed that he could be as adroit a strategist as he was an intrepid and audacious foe. He sacrificed the remnants of Broussier's brave division to the common good (the handful of survivors joined them the next day), and retreated during the night in silence towards the Dnieper, the unevenness of the ground serving as a shelter to the troops, while Broussier's fire kept the enemy's attention distracted.

His stratagem promised success, notwithstanding the moonlight, when suddenly a Russian corps in marching order barred the way. One of the Polish officers on his staff went before the Russian commander, and, with rare presence of mind, convinced him that he had a detachment of Russian soldiers executing a secret movement;

and the fleeing corps, thanks to his trick, escaped to safety after a most hazardous night's march.

Eugene's task did not diminish in difficulty or hardship. Marshal Ney, setting out two days after him from Smolensk, according to Napoleon's mistaken order, being attacked in his turn by fifty thousand Russians, and escaping from them, thanks to prodigies of valour and skill, called promptly for help. Eugene, without taking time to rest after his own fatigues, promptly extended a helping hand to the brave Marshal.

The meeting of the two heroes under these tragic circumstances presented a picture of simple and touching grandeur. This is Constant's version of the subject: —

"To Prince Eugene was given the honour of going to meet Marshal Ney with a corps of four thousand brave men. Marshal Mortier had disputed this favour with him, for among these illustrious men there were never any but noble rivalries. The danger was great. The Prince's cannon was a signal understood by the Marshal, who was to reply by firing twice by platoons. The two corps met. The Prince and the Marshal no sooner met than they fell into each other's arms; the former, it is said, wept for joy!"

III.

At last this demoralised army reached the shores of the Beresina, to find that the Russians had cut away all the bridges. General Elbe's soldiers repaired the damage; and Napoleon, accompanied by Prince Eugene and Marshal Ney, each with a following of two thousand men and their different staffs, with the remnants of the other regiments, were enabled to leave the accursed river behind them, across whose turbulent waters captivity had lain in wait for them. This army, more than sixty thousand strong when it had crossed the Niemen in June, had fallen in five months to such a degree of misery that they congratulated themselves on having been able to cross the Beresina without falling into the hands of the enemy.

On the following day, the 28th, they were again forced into a bloody but victorious battle, although less than thirty thousand French found themselves confronted by seventy-five thousand Russians.

During this desperate combat, the unarmed rabble which had followed the army's footsteps precipitated themselves with such frenzy on the bridge destined for foot-passengers that a large number of them fell into the water, clinging to the cakes of floating ice, trying to escape the awful death threatening them, and adding a scene of horror to that of the desolation all around them.

To cut off pursuit by the Russians, they burned the bridges behind them on the next day, the 29th, as soon as the army had passed over. It was necessary to abandon a number of wounded and of women and stragglers, as prey for the Cossacks, who in their cruelty did not hesitate to plunge their lances into these defenceless victims. As though this spectacle of itself was not pitiful enough, they saw many of these unfortunate creatures throw themselves into the icy waters of the Beresina to escape the flames.

During the horrors of this retreat from Russia, all communications were intercepted. Eugene was unable to acquaint the Vice-Queen with his movements. Not until December 1st, was he fortunate enough to start a courier to Paris carrying the following letter, — a letter silent on the subject of so many bloody struggles, so many irreparable disasters: —

ILLIJA, December 1, 1812, Evening.

At last communications are all opened, for which God be thanked! It is too cruel to be obliged to remain so long without sending any news or receiving any from one's loved ones. We are all very much fatigued with our long marches, and the cold, which reddens the end of our noses in a terrible manner. My health has not suffered, fortunately, but I have my whole household on the sick-list. The Emperor is well, and he is very good to me. He was so extremely kind as to write to the Empress Marie Louise to send her news of me at a time when it was impossible for me to do it myself.

What agonies the poor Princess suffered during the fortnight of her husband's enforced silence! — two weeks which anxiety transformed into years. She received, it is true, indirect news of Eugene by the Duc de Bassano, who had been stationed at Wilna to watch over the communications of the Grand Army; but was not such news more distressing for the loving wife's heart than silence itself?

WILNA, December, 1812.

MADAME, — The Viceroy has doubtless not written to Your Royal Highness for several days. Parties of Cossacks momentarily intercepted all communications. An officer who left the headquarters at Zanishg near Zembrü, on November 29, has assured me that the

Viceroy continues in excellent health; and all my letters tell me that he is often with the Emperor, and that this campaign will have added, if such a thing be possible, to the attachment His Majesty has for him.   I am, with respect, Madame, etc.

The débris of the Grand Army arrived at Smorghoni on December 5.   Napoleon, who for some days had been cherishing the secret idea of leaving the army, called his generals and staff officers together.   Overcome by the most profound emotion, he announced his immediate departure for Paris.   This resolution of Napoleon's has been much criticised, with more blame than approval.   The truth is, that the conspiracy of Malet, of which he had just received word, showed him with what facility an audacious general had been able almost to overthrow his empire, by spreading the rumour of his death.   He could thus gauge the danger to his crown if, his present disaster being known, Europe should rise up *en masse* and shut him out of his domains.

His anxiety was very great, and it must be acknowledged justifiable.   Having Poland and Germany to cross, it was necessary for him to set out without delay, and in the greatest secrecy, before a suspicion of the entire destruction of the immense army upon which his power alone rested, had reached his enemies. Napoleon a prisoner of the Allies, was in truth the Empire and France destroyed!

To return to Paris in great haste; to re-establish himself firmly on his throne; to prepare new resources, and reorganise an army to hold his own against Europe, which his disastrous defeats in Russia could not fail to call to arms against him, — such was and such should have been his sole preoccupation.

He therefore determined to abandon this army incapable of defending his prestige; but, before leaving it to its fate, he drew up his famous Twenty-ninth Bulletin, so celebrated for the frankness with which he pictures the condition of the army in Russia. The passages of the bulletin which I am about to quote throw light in a startling manner upon the terrible trials to which Eugene and the marshals, so much more than Napoleon himself, had been subjected, — trials which were about to be so painfully prolonged for the Viceroy, obliged later on to assume almost the entire responsibility of this ghostly army, so far from France, and in a hostile country.

Speaking of the terrible cold and its awful

effects upon the cavalry, Napoleon traces this
picture: —

" The cold weather came upon us on the 7th, and
suddenly grew in intensity, until on the 16th the thermometer marked sixteen and eighteen degrees below
zero.   The roads were sheets of ice ; the cavalry horses
and the teams of the artillery waggons perished every
night, not by hundreds, but by thousands, especially the
French and German horses.   More than thirty thousand
horses died in a few days; our cavalry found themselves
on foot, our artillery and transports without teams.   We
were obliged to abandon and destroy a good part of
our guns, ammunition, and even provisions."

On the subject of the condition of the army
itself, the Emperor adds : —

" This army, in such good condition on the 6th, was
very different after the 14th, and almost without cavalry,
artillery, or transports.   Without cavalry we could not
clear the road a quarter of a league away.   Without
artillery we did not dare risk an encounter, and stand
firm in our places.   We were obliged to march in such
a manner as not to be forced into a battle which our
lack of ammunition hindered us from desiring.

" These difficulties, joined to the sudden and excessive
cold, rendered our situation a sorry one.   Men whom
nature had not sufficiently steeled to put them above
the goads of fate and fortune, were dazed, lost their
spirits, their good-nature, and could dream of nothing

but miseries and catastrophes. Those who had been created in a superior mould preserved their gaiety and their ordinary manners, and could see a new glory in the difficulties they were called upon to overcome."

Further on, he gives Eugene credit for his wonderful military services : —

"The enemy, seeing on the roadside the traces of this awful calamity which had struck the French army, endeavoured to profit by it. They surrounded the columns by their Cossacks, who, like the Arabs in the deserts, carried away all the trains and carriages which they could lay hands upon. This miserable cavalry, which makes no noise, and which is not capable of riding down a company of mountebanks, was redoubtable from force of circumstances. Nevertheless, the enemy was made to repent of all the serious attempts he had undertaken. He was overthrown by the Viceroy, before whom he had planted himself, and lost a number of men."

IV.

Napoleon transferred the command of the armies to Murat, who so soon after abandoned it, — the first defection towards one to whom he owed a crown.

Eugene, with the clairvoyance of an honest heart, had realised Murat's fickle character. The latter but half dissimulated his sentiments towards the Viceroy, — sentiments which were anything but cordial. Eugene, on his part, very frankly asked Napoleon to relieve him of his command.

The letter which he wrote to the Emperor on this subject is a model of military abnegation. The hand which writes it is easily seen to be that of a soldier without fear and without reproach, in whose heart the sentiment of duty overtops all personal considerations : —

December 5, 1812.

SIRE, — It is not for me to endeavour to penetrate Your Majesty's will; but as it is probable that Your Majesty will not delay in returning to your duty as Emperor of the French nation, and as your intention has been to leave me with the army under the King of Naples, I take the liberty of claiming a new proof of your kindness towards me. May I make bold enough to ask you for an order returning me to Italy at a time most convenient to yourself? In case Your Majesty should wish to leave me with the army, I will remain as long as it suits you, and I will continue to serve you with the same zeal and the same devotion !

Napoleon, knowing how indispensable Eugene's firmness and his organising genius were to the army, replied simply : —

MY DEAR SON, — I received your letter. Do your duty, and rely on me. I am always the same for you. Never doubt my paternal sentiments.

When the Emperor wrote in these terms, how well he showed his knowledge of his step-son's character!

The latter, notwithstanding his repugnance to serving under Murat, immediately submitted. The supreme commander so willed it; he would remain at no matter what cost! This decision he announced to his wife in the following terms:

BIVOUAC NEAR OCHMIANA, December 6, 1812.

Good-evening, my dear Augusta. I am well, in spite of the excessive cold weather we are having. I think the thermometer stands at 18 degrees below zero. You no doubt know by this time that the Emperor has left the army to go to Paris. He is impressed with the fact that his presence is necessary there. The rest of us remain at our posts. I hope, however, if we do no active work this winter, I may return to Milan for a time. I am anxious to do so for more than one reason; but as to leaving here at present, that will be very ill advised of me. Our duty is at our post, whether that duty be hard or easy. Adieu, my very dear Augusta. I shall be at Wilna day after to-morrow, from which place I shall send Allemagne (the Prince's aide-de-camp) with letters and despatches. The poor devil is nearly worn out. I thought he was really frozen to-day.

The army, still harassed by the Cossacks, finally reached Wilna. But could one give the name of army to the miserable and disbanded troops of men, or rather wandering phantoms, whose only thoughts were to pile up a few logs of wood and set fire to them in order to warm their frozen limbs, to swallow a little bread and whiskey to sustain their emaciated bodies, and to crouch in some sheltered spot against the cold until chased from it by the lances of their enemies?

Eugene turned his thoughts from so much misery to dream of his far-distant happiness at the side of his loved companion, whose every heartbeat was for him. The hope of a peaceful future beside his own hearthstone, of which he spoke in such glowing terms, aided him, joined to his energetic sentiments of duty, to brave his misery and present sufferings.

From Rankoni, near Wilna, he writes on December 8th: —

"My health is good; but, like all the rest of us, I am very much in need of repose. I sent Allemagne to you night before last. The poor fellow needed a change. He could not stand much more. I could give him no presents for you nor for the children, for I have lost all our waggons and all our horses. I left at least twenty domestics behind us, who were too exhausted to follow. All our fatigues and sorrows will be forgotten as soon as we are once more with our families. Every day teaches us more clearly that true happiness exists only there. Embrace my four little angels for me. I do this daily in spirit as at every moment of my life I think of the happiness which Heaven bestowed upon me in uniting our destinies. Let us hope to be soon reunited, nevermore to part!"

Wilna, towards which every eye had been turned as a haven of rest, was to be the theatre of a new disaster, added to so many others in the condition of general demoralisation caused by this interminable retreat and by Napoleon's absence. There was, so to speak, no one in command. Throwing themselves against the city gates, the soldiers, crazed by suffering, rushed to the stores, where they stole provisions, clothing, and liquors. On the 9th, at nightfall, Platow's Cossacks suddenly appeared. Ney, old General Lefèbvre, Eugene, and some of the other generals, fighting as common soldiers, succeeded in rallying a few hundred men around them, who repulsed the Cossacks and assured a short respite, during which the French evacuated Wilna!

Alas! nearly twenty thousand men, wounded and sick, or worn out with fatigue, were left behind, the men preferring to fall into the hands of the Russians, rather than continue this deadly march without shelter or food. They retreated from Wilna to Kowno, where six months before

Napoleon had first set foot on Russian soil, at the head of six hundred and twenty-five thousand soldiers.

What a heart-rending contrast! The army which entered Kowno was nothing more than a band of thirty-five hundred men marching in such disorder that the Marshals, gathered in a war council, were forced to confess that the army had definitely ceased to exist.

The following few lines show to what a condition of desolation our soldiers had been reduced. Do they not give us the impression of a ship in distress, wrecked amid icebergs, and lost to the rest of the world?

KOWNO, December 12, 1812.

These past few days the thermometer has stood at twenty-one and even twenty-five degrees. This has been very disastrous for us. I am in a condition of indescribable anger against Allemagne, who started out four days ago. I found him yesterday on the highways, having lost his horses, his servants, and his despatches. That means my correspondence for Milan for the past month.

That same day Eugene made the attempt to send his news by the way of Paris. The pictures he traces of the ravages wrought by the fatigue undergone, and the cold suffered in his own immediate military household, are heart-rending.

KOWNO, December 12, 1812.

MY DEAREST AUGUSTA, — I can easily understand
all that you are suffering. It is to be hoped, however, that Heaven will grow weary of keeping us much
longer separated, and that we can be reunited. The
cold is terrible to-day, and every day we lose some of
our friends and companions. Lacroix was obliged to
remain at Wilna; his condition was such we could not
transport him. Bataille and Pétrus are in the hospital,
very ill. Leroy and Brochier are suffering intensely.
If this lasts much longer, I shall certainly be left entirely alone without any staff.

Eugene concentrated all his efforts in endeavouring to rally his organised soldiers, so completely crushed by this frightful temperature, and
planning an attack on the Cossacks, who pursued
them relentlessly.

It was a herculean task to try to re-establish a
little order in the broken ranks·of these miserable creatures, a great number of whom were
unarmed or invalids.

At last they reached the borders of Poland,
but at the price of nameless fatigues and sufferings, the sight of which moved Eugene deeply.

Obliged to leave his Mameluke Pétrus behind
him, among many others, he sadly expatiated on
this brave fellow's sad fate. Though witnessing

so many scenes of carnage and death, the sensibilities of this noble heart were so little blunted that the abandonment of a poor sick attendant touched him deeply: —

WIRBALLEN, December 15, 1812.

We are on the frontiers of Poland and Russia. It seems it will be in this latter country, and near the Vistula, that we shall halt and take up our winter-quarters, and, indeed, there is great necessity for us to get some rest. The enemy pursued us with a large number of men as far as Wilna. From Wilna to Kowno, we were only slightly molested by a few cavalry and artillery. I hope they themselves will be too much fatigued to follow us farther, and will not attempt to cross the Niemen after us. I was obliged to leave poor Pétrus (the Mameluke) behind at Kowno. He was beyond transportation. I very much fear I shall lose him. I recommended him to the people who lodged me, and left him plenty of money. I am feeling well amid all our fatigues. . . .

V.

Poland crossed, and Germany at last reached! From his first stopping-place in Prussia, the Viceroy wrote to the Princess to reassure her on his account, and to make her the sharer of his hope of soon enjoying near her his well-earned repose. He announces to her that she must no longer tremble at the recital of his combats, his marches, and his fatigues, and ends with a burst of French humour which finds something to laugh about even in the midst of the greatest trouble: —

GUMBINNEM, December 17, 1812.

At last we are in Prussia, my very dear Augusta, and I will despatch Fortis with my letters. He will make good time. We have been in retreat since leaving Wilna, and the enemy has only followed us with his cavalry and artillery. I do not think any length of time will pass without some important military move being made. It is probable that the Emperor will order me back to Italy, and that is all I desire in this world. Fortis will tell you of all who are in good health here, and of those who are ill; and there are many of the latter. I have been fortunate enough so far to find myself among the former. It will please you to know this, in spite of all the battles we have fought, all the fatigues we have undergone. Adieu.

P. S. To amuse your ladies-in-waiting, tell them that very probably half their friends will return without noses or ears. Everything freezes here. We have already had it at 24 below.

Writing the same day to his private secretary, Baron Darnay, towards whom he had not the same motives for hiding the gloomy truth, in a few lines he gives a simple and truthful picture of the greatest military disaster of modern times. The cry which escapes him at the end of his letter is worthy of this generous, heroic, tender soul, so far above human ambitions : —

"I am sending Fortis to Milan. Question him well, my dear Darnay; and if he is frank in his replies, you will know all we have suffered during the past few months. The climate has destroyed us. Of that grand and beautiful army a mere handful of men remain. Our losses are immense. The sights we have under our eyes every day are heart-rending. Our friends and our comrades are dying along the roadside from misery, fatigue, and cold. The Commissary Joubert died three days ago. The Italians are dropping down like flies. The Royal Guard numbers only two hundred men. Happy will be those who once more see their firesides! This is my only aim in life now! I desire no more glory; it is obtained at too great a cost. Adieu! Yours for ever."

Marching towards Marienwerder to reach his winter-quarters, the Viceroy visited the battlefields of Eylau and Friedland, — those two great victories of the campaign of 1807, which he had so deeply regretted not participating in.

From Eylau, December 22, he sent the Princess a modest and late New Year's gift, — a little spoon "which had been found at the bottom of a box he had thought to be lost."

"We are going," he writes to his wife, "to commence a New Year. I ardently hope that it will be happier than this one; that is to say, that we may be reunited, never to be separated again."

He adds this doleful refrain : —

" Here we have cold and snow; the inhabitants try to console us for our sufferings by telling us that it is the most rigorous winter they have had in thirty years. We made a good choice, did we not?"

Then he winds up with this joke, a little military in its character, but to which the surrounding circumstances give a singular flavour of Gallic gallantry : —

" These past few days eight officers of my staff have had their feet and noses frozen. You cannot say much in favour of men who have come out of an affair like this with one foot and no nose. The longest were the first to fall."

At Marienwerder, Eugene was enabled to enjoy a little repose, as the Russians, exhausted themselves, did not dare continue their pursuit on German soil. A number of stragglers and those left behind joined the army by degrees, and soon brought the numbers up to two thousand, and this was the corps that was noted for being in such fine condition when they first crossed the Niemen. In the midst of this calm, the Prince was seized with a sentiment of regret evoked by the thoughts of the sweetness of his family life, which finally became the constant object of his dreams.

MARIENWERDER, December 28, 1812.

I reached here the evening of the day before yesterday, my dear Augusta; and it is now my pleasant duty to concern myself as to your health. At last we have reached the end of our journey. It seems we are to take up our winter-quarters here. It will be very wearisome, I am afraid; but we must have courage, and, above all, patience. I received your dear letter and the warm clothing. I distributed them as you desired, among my officers. I was very happy on learning that our little family were in good health, for I think of them constantly these days. I am of the opinion that the Emperor will not leave me here in inactivity all winter, with so few men. Would you believe it, my dear, that out of my Grand Army corps, there only remain to me two thousand men, one-half of whom are wounded. This is for you alone. Adieu, my very dear Augusta. Let us hope that one day we will forget all our troubles in each other's arms.

Eugene remained a fortnight at Marienwerder. He employed the time which he could spare from the cares of his little band in attending to the affairs of Italy, as he had indeed done to the best of his ability during this unfortunate campaign. He was an indefatigable worker; and he was able by the 3d of January, 1813, to send the Emperor a long and detailed account of the actual condition of his kingdom.

But it was not the moment to expatiate merely on the affairs of the kingdom. The situation was more dangerous than ever. Desertions were numerous. The Prussians declared themselves on the side of the enemy, and threatened the débris of the Grand Army. Eugene's situation, surrounded by open and secret enemies, was very critical. In his retreat from Grandenz, the Prussian garrison had evinced signs of a hostility they were at no pains to conceal; but the heroic Viceroy had great faith in his star. No matter how great was the peril in which he found himself, nothing could daunt his confidence in the future. At the sound of the battle, the soldier in him awoke, proud, ironical, and calm; and he wrote as though he attached little importance to this recommencement of hostilities.

SCHWETZ, January 13, 1813.

Just two words, my well-beloved Augusta. I received Provari, and he handed me your welcome letter of the 1st of this year. You are right to trust in Providence, and to believe that God watches over me. I was born lucky, and I never appreciated my happiness since uniting my destiny to yours, more than I do at this present time.

We left our quarters at Marienwerder yesterday. I have received orders from the King to repair to Posen. We had a skirmish with the Cossacks yesterday. In the evening, as we were getting into position before Nenenberg, they had the impertinence to try to worry us again; but I attacked them at once, and a single battalion was all that was needed to send them back to the Vistula. It was very comical to see five hundred of those strapping fellows pursued over the ice by our small soldiers. We killed several and captured a dozen horses. To-day we have been very quiet. I am well, except for a slight inflammation, which has almost passed away.

At that moment the Prince was on the verge of one of the most critical epochs of his life.

CHAPTER VIII.

Departure of King Murat. — Eugene as Commander-in-Chief of the Grand Army. — Difficulties of the Situation. — The Retreat on the Oder. — Discouragement of the Army. — Efforts of the Prince to Reorganise it. — The Retreat on the Elbe. — Return of the Emperor. — Eugene at Lützen. — Departure for Italy.

I.

I HAVE now reached one of the most remarkable events of the Prince's career, — an epoch in which he fully merited Napoleon and France's recognition. Charged with an extremely difficult mission, and one bringing no glory to him, he accomplished it in such a manner as to force men to honour him, even personal enemies such as Marshal Marmont. It was Eugene who, in a country openly unfriendly, in the midst of an over-excited and hostile population, had proudly led the débris of the Grand Army across Germany.

As we have seen, Napoleon, fearing for the stability of the dynasty created by him, had, on setting out so suddenly for Paris, transmitted the supreme command to his brother-in-law, Murat, King of Naples.

But Murat was too fond of his crown, too much occupied by his personal interests in Italy, to devote himself long to the ungrateful task of rallying the disbanded soldiers, rearming and reorganising them. On January 17th, Murat suddenly announced to Eugene his intention of setting out for Naples; and he transferred the command of the army to him, — a command which Eugene justly considered he had no right to accept from any hand but Napoleon's.

But rather than leave the army without a head, the Prince provisionally accepted this command, which Murat abandoned.

POSEN, January 17, 1813.

MY DEAR AUGUSTA, — I have most unlooked-for news to announce to you. After my departure for Marienwerder, King Murat wrote me to join him at Posen. I had hardly reached here before he informed me he intended to resign his command of the army, and set out without waiting for the Emperor's decision. He is ill, and no longer desires the responsibility. He wished to transfer the command to me, but I was not willing to receive it from him; but as he insisted upon going, I was obliged to accept the command provisionally. It is a delicate position for me; but I offer it as a last proof of my devotion to the Emperor. Everything here is in great confusion; and I assure you, my good Augusta, that I have a terrible task before me. I dare not hope to come out covered with glory; but at least I shall be said to have had the courage to accept it, and I hope to get credit for not having abandoned it.

Adieu, my dear Augusta; what troubles me most is that I cannot write to you oftener, as I lack time.

To Napoleon on the same day he wrote: —

SIRE, — I have the honour to announce to Your Majesty that the King really set out this morning at three o'clock. Yesterday evening the Prince de Neu-châtel [Berthier] and myself exhausted all possible reasons for persuading him to remain. There being no Marshal of the Empire here, and I being the only lieutenant in Your Majesty's service present, I have provisionally assumed command until Your Majesty can send some general-in-chief to relieve me. I am going to try and gather together a few thousand men to at least open communication by way of the Oder with Warsaw. I deeply regret not having twenty thousand men at my disposal; for I am convinced that by reinforcing our right and surrounding Warsaw, the enemy will abandon his idea of attempting any serious move in that direction in the next campaign. At the present moment I unfortunately have not a single well-organised division.

Napoleon, who understood men, and who had just had in his Russian experience ample occasion to appreciate Eugene, replied at once: —

FONTAINEBLEAU, January 22, 1813.

MY SON, — Take the command of the Grand Army. I regret not leaving it with you on my departure. I flatter myself you would have retreated more quietly, and I should not have experienced such immense losses. The harm done is past remedy.

You will write me in detail every day.

The next day Napoleon reiterates his satisfaction that the command is in Eugene's hands. The greatest captain of modern times thus shows in what high esteem he holds the military capabilities of the young Viceroy, to whom he has confided the heavy responsibilities of a Commander-in-Chief, in exceptionally difficult circumstances.

FONTAINEBLEAU, January 23, 1813.

MY SON, — I received your letter of the 16th. I have already written to you that I am pleased to know the command of the army is in your hands. I find the King's conduct very extraordinary. He is a brave man on the battle-field, but he lacks tact and moral courage.

King Louis of Holland expresses himself thus on this subject. He was a most impartial judge, from the fact that his quarrel with his brother, since the Emperor had taken his crown from him, had kept him aloof from the intrigues of the Court and the jealousies of the staff officers.

"The Emperor left the army and gave the command to the King of Naples, who a short time afterwards resigned it into the hands of the Viceroy of Italy, so that he could return to Naples. By this act he partially sacrificed to his own whims the interest of his own kingdom, the general interests of the allies of France, and, above all, the glory and preservation of the precious débris of this illustrious army. The remnants of the Grand Army have performed wonderful deeds of valour under the order of the Viceroy, who can flatter himself upon having had the grandest and most difficult commission to fulfil, and upon having performed his duty with as much prudence and glory as success."

II.

Napoleon's confidence was justified, as will be seen from the following letter. I do not really know if, in all the Prince's correspondence, there is a more beautiful letter than the one I am about to have the pleasure of transcribing for the reader. It is charming in its delicacy, devotion, and unutterable tenderness.

POSEN, January 18, 1813.

MY DEAR AND GOOD AUGUSTA,—I am up to my neck in work, and I can assure you that I must work. I received your letter of January 8th, at reveille this morning. I am not angry at you for the request you made to

the Emperor; but it is not the moment to speak of my
return, or our happiness in seeing each other again.
You must understand how much His Majesty is afflicted
in his heart by all that has passed; and so many are
abandoning him now that it is just in such painful and
difficult situations that one should show the most devotion, courage, and resignation.   You, who have so much
of all three, must not lose any now.   Yet one more
effort, and I predict we shall at last enjoy the happiness
of being reunited and tranquil.   Adieu, my very dear
Augusta.   I could not for a moment permit myself to
think of such a thing as a journey here for you.   Besides, we are not settled; and then the season, and, still
again, the children.   Patience; let us love each other
more, if such a thing is in our power.

The Princess, whose lofty soul was in such
perfect communion of sentiments with those of
her husband, had implored the Emperor to give
her back her husband, whose continued absence
caused her such anxiety; but she had made this
request before she knew the King of Naples had
abandoned the command of the army.

As soon as she learned of Murat's departure,
she restrained her hopes in face of the perilous
greatness of the duty to be accomplished.

Eugene himself, on the 20th of January, 1813,
writes openly of the difficulties of the heavy task
which he had assumed from pure devotion to

the Emperor. He could not refrain from a slight touch of irony on the subject of the pretext put forward by Murat of "sickness" as an excuse for the strange abandonment of his command.

"I found everything here in the greatest disorder, every one thinking of nothing but saving himself. No one seems to know where the troops are, even. I think I shall have accomplished a great deal if I succeed in quieting the minds of, and in putting a little order into, the regiments. I hope it will not be said that it is the desire of glory which made me assume the command of the army; for it is from pure devotion to the Emperor, and it would be impossible to accept a more difficult task. I have not heard from His Majesty the Emperor yet. Let me know if it is true that the King passed you by on his road to Naples, for he told us he would rest some time with the King of Westphalia [Jerome]; and for a sick man it is doing pretty well to go in one journey straight to Naples. It must be confessed that the Emperor is but shabbily treated by his own family. I hope this last act will open his eyes. . . ."

One of the most amiable phases of Eugene's character was his solicitude towards the humblest of those who approached him. The high and charitable simplicity of his heart did not admit,

in the expression of his sentiments, the egotisti-
cal, worldly conventions of caste.

I cited one example in the forced abandonment
of Pétrus, the Mameluke. I am pleased to be able
to recall another incident in the postscript of the
following letter : —

> "I have a great deal of work, but I do it with pleas-
> ure, especially if by doing so I can make the Emperor
> know his true friends. We have made no movements
> of any kind yet; but I dare not flatter myself too much,
> and I am afraid the enemy will oblige us to retreat
> behind the Oder, in which case this poor Poland will
> be occupied by the Russians.
> "P. S. Michel's son died day before yesterday. It
> has made me very sad, for he was a good *valet-de-pied.*"

Napoleon's marks of confidence had greatly
encouraged Eugene in the accomplishment of his
painful duties. The detailed instructions from
the Emperor relative to the reorganisation and
revictualling of the army, proved a precious help
to him.

Even at this period the vacillation of the Prince
von Schwarzenberg inspired Eugene's prudent
sagacity with doubts of the fidelity of the Austrians. At the same time he conceived the same
suspicions with regard to the Saxons, who amply

justified them in the bloody battle of Leipzig.
However, in the midst of these heavy cares, his
greatest uneasiness perhaps came to him from
Italy. The Princess's failing health caused him
inexpressible anxiety.

POSEN, January 25, 1813.

. . . Your letter of the 15th proves to me that your
health is not as good as you say it is, and I am worried.
Be careful of yourself, my good Augusta. Make yourself easy as to my position, and hope that our lucky
star will soon reunite us. I am working a great deal;
but it is a pleasure to me, as I can already see the
good results of my work. Order has been re-established,
and the men who ran the fastest are commencing to
blush at their conduct, and I can predict a great change
soon. . . .

However, the situation still remained grave, on
account of the general discouragement. Eugene
was not sanguine.

" Sire," he writes to Napoleon from Posen, February
2, 1813, "I received your orders relative to the
command of the Duc d'Elchingen [Ney]. I have
already had the honour of notifying you that the Marshal had left Elbing for Magdeburg, from which place
he had demanded permission to return to France. This
permission being granted him, he must by this time be
in Paris. Marshal Ney quitted the army, fatigued, dis-
contented with King Murat, and loudly declaring that it

was oftener than necessary his turn to lead the advance
or rear guard. I cannot explain to Your Majesty to
what an extent the general discouragement in the army
has spread since we left Wilna. Very few generals remain at their posts. Would Your Majesty believe, for
instance, that General X., . . . who is a brave soldier,
did not think himself safe at Custrin, and has retired to
Berlin? He has not come to see me yet, notwithstanding the three orders I have sent him to do so. I have
written to him for the last time, and if he does not
report in forty-eight hours, I shall court-martial him.
I hope not to be obliged to resort to these extreme
measures; but I feel it my duty to do this, as I must
make a severe example of some one for the purpose
of re-establishing a little order."

The most delicate part of his heavy task was
to elevate the *morale* of the troops, who had
deteriorated so sadly amid all the hardships endured. He succeeded in this, thanks to his
energetic and constant efforts. With the reinforcements he gradually gathered together, he
performed the miracle of turning over to the
Emperor, when the latter resumed command of
the forces in the spring, a good army, solid,
and animated with true military ardour. But for
the present he was obliged to retreat, always to
retreat, — he, the enthusiastic young chief, accustomed to pursue the enemy and conquer him.

He foresaw the coming impossibility of holding Poland, and the painful obligation of seeking a refuge beyond the Oder, — a harsh necessity which deeply wounded his soldier's vanity.

POSEN, February 2, 1813.

. . . I am obliged to be very severe if I wish to succeed in establishing any kind of discipline. You cannot imagine how disorganised the whole army is. The Russians, who had apparently ceased hostilities, have commenced to move on us; and if this movement continues, I shall be forced to retreat beyond the Oder, which will annoy me very much, for I have not made a retrograde step for the last eighteen days. Well, in a very few days I shall know just where I stand. I hope soon to be either in Paris or Munich; but I cannot know anything positive in this respect, and it will be at least a month before there is any degree of certainty as to my future movements. I will make no more plans; they all turn out badly. I only want to love you all my life, for in that consists my whole happiness.

The principal division of the Russian army, for a while stationary on the borders of Poland, had been steadily advancing for several days, the second corps following in its footsteps, whilst Prince von Schwarzenberg with his Austrians retreated in a manner which was anything but reassuring to Eugene, and rendered his position still more critical. But well he seemed to forget the agonies of his command when, in terms breathing so much noble simplicity, he said to his wife : —

POSEN, February 4, 1813.

The courier arrived this morning with your letters, and they afforded me great pleasure. Rest easy on my account. I am gladly recompensed for all my troubles by your tenderness, by my family happiness, and the good opinion which you have of me.

Eugene, with the meagre resources at his disposal, was enabled to hold his own at Posen for a month ; but that was the maximum effort of resistance which was permitted him. At last he was obliged to abandon this last rallying-point, and retreat.

Each backward step, it is true, brought him a little nearer to that beautiful Italy, where such tender ties bound him; but the proud soldier silenced the loving husband, and the only feeling he experienced was one of chagrin at being obliged to retreat before the enemy.

POSEN, February 10, 1813.

It is probable that I shall leave this city to-morrow or the day after. The Russians are advancing on us in great numbers, and all we can do is to retreat beyond the Oder. I hope, however, that this will be our last halt. I know nothing definite as yet in our grand schemes of being together in the spring; only one thing is certain, and that is the ardent longing I constantly experience for their realisation.

The decimated troops who had recrossed the Niemen under Eugene's command were, without doubt, already in a measure reorganised and augmented in numbers; but how miserable were they still, in comparison with the immense numbers of Russians and their allies, pressing forward against them! And yet the Prince, with the miserable remnants of this once glorious army under his hand, held his head up proudly in face of his enemies.

February 13, 1813.

As I predicted, I was obliged to leave Posen to approach nearer to my reinforcements. I have twenty thousand men and one thousand horses two days' march behind me, and with these I fear nothing. I only left Posen at the last moment, and not until several thousand Cossacks had cut off my communications. Poor little Janois (a domestic of Eugene's) was taken prisoner yesterday evening by them. I had sent him ahead to prepare my lodgings.

The minutely detailed reports which the Viceroy sent constantly to the Emperor, on the military situation, showed not only his indefatigable

energy, but also the perfect confidence which
Napoleon reposed in the young general only
thirty-two years old, whom he had placed in au-
thority over old and illustrious marshals like
Davout, Prince d'Eckmühl, Victor, the Duc de
Bellum, Augereau, and the Duc de Castiglione.

III.

The defence and provisioning of the fortresses
of Cüstrin, Glogau, and Spandau, which the
French held in Germany, and which Napoleon
desired to retain, added to the difficulties and
responsibilities of the Viceroy, who was obliged
to attend to them, and at the same time to maintain a calm and well-managed retreat before an
enemy of crushing superiority.

MESERITZ, February 17, 1813.

I have rested here for the past two days, my dear
. Augusta, notwithstanding the reports which have been
brought to me that the enemy would reach the Oder
before me; and I was wise in not believing them, for I
have positive news this morning that all this gossip was
false. The enemy is still advancing but slowly, and we
are retiring in the same manner. I hope he will be prudent enough not to attack us this side of the Oder.
If, by chance, Prussia fail us, I think we shall be obliged

to gain the shores of the Elbe as promptly as possible. You can see by this that my position is not a brilliant one. I do not dissimulate all that is painful and difficult. You may be sure that I shall not lose courage, and that I shall always do my duty.

He had only two good reasons to dread a defection on the part of Prussia, whose king more and more readily lent his ear to the warlike counsels which were constantly offered him. I select the following passage from a voluminous report, dated February 18 : —

" The ill feeling which dominates Prussia at this moment is only too apparent. The authorities refuse to distribute provisions to our troops. The peasants leave their houses as our columns approach, so as not to be obliged to feed our soldiers. And when the enemy appears, the burgomasters point out the movements of our troops, and the gendarmes go so far as to guard our prisoners taken by the Cossacks."

The enemy marched forward even to the walls of Berlin, and Eugene was obliged to hasten towards this capital to lend a helping hand to the French garrison, which had occupied it since the commencement of the Russian campaign. This garrison, with Augereau at its head, though seriously menaced, had put on ·so brave a front that it had deceived the Allies as to its strength.

" The enemy," Eugene says in a report to Napoleon, dated Berlin, February 22d, " has advanced as far as Berlin, and day before yesterday some eighty Cossacks entered the city and threw the inhabitants into a condition of terror. The stand taken by the Duc de Castiglione [Augereau], who had assembled his garrison and placed his artillery and batteries in the principal streets, caused the enemy to promptly retire. They retreated to Charlottenburg, and sent out small parties of from twenty-five to forty horses skirmishing over the open country. On this occasion the burgher's guard of Berlin behaved admirably, and in the most efficient manner helped to re-establish order. The populace were very ugly. Officers and single soldiers were maltreated by them. Learning this news at Fürstenwald, and knowing that Marshal Augereau had no cavalry at his command to chase the Cossacks away, I set out this morning with the cavalry of the Guard, and, by making extra quick time, I reached here before four o'clock. The enemy was warned of our arrival, and has not shown around the city except for a few Cossacks. . . .

" To-morrow before daybreak, I shall send my cavalry out into the open country, to chase them from the vicinity of the city. "

From the Berlin Suburb of Köpenick, where he had established his headquarters, Eugene hastened the reorganisation of his army and incorporated the reinforcements received, and the troops of the Berlin garrison. He thus found himself at the head of more than twenty-six thousand men.

Between the threats of insurrection by the populace and the announcement of the commencement of hostilities by the whole Russian army, the Prince's position in Berlin became daily more and more critical. Thousands of Cossacks scoured the country, cutting off communication, intercepting convoys of provisions, and even succeeding in destroying several isolated detachments. But notwithstanding his constant efforts to augment his defences, Eugene, deprived of his cavalry, could make no headway against the continual insults heaped upon him by these barbarous horsemen, who had so often fled before that grand French cavalry now buried under Russia's frozen fields : —

SCHÖNEBERG, NEAR BERLIN, February 28, 1813.

The enemy appears to desire a renewal of hostilities, as the first columns have passed the Oder to-day. I am not speaking of the parties of the Cossacks, who have already thrown themselves upon us. They do not count. I am beginning to reinforce my army. I have thirty thousand bayonets and eighty pieces of artillery under me; but unhappily I need cavalry, which is the most essential of all. Lauriston has just reached the Elbe with forty thousand men, but he has no cavalry either. The King of Prussia has not yet declared himself against us, and I am anxiously awaiting news from Breslau [the provisional residence of the Prussian Court]. You can judge from this, my beloved, how busy I am, and how difficult my position is.

The fatal Russian campaign had not only produced irreparable losses in men and horses, in *matériel* and prestige, but the sufferings undergone and the disorder of the retreat had also overthrown the strongest wills. A great many officers were far from fulfilling their duties with the devotion and untiring energy displayed by Eugene.

He, in fact, exposed the conduct of a chief of battalion named Cicerow to Napoleon. This officer, given the charge of defending a very important position commanding the passage of the communications with Dresden and Leipzig, had allowed himself to be so intimidated by the approach of the enemy as to evacuate his post without sufficient military reasons. To make an example of this officer, the Prince asked Napoleon to " punish his pusillanimity by sending him to the guard-house and returning him to the ranks."

But Napoleon looked upon these acts in a much more rigorous manner, as the following shows : —

" My Son," — he writes from Paris to the Viceroy, March 2, 1813, — " I received your letter of February 25. I am astonished that you did not have this officer who left his post, notwithstanding his obvious duty, arrested, tried by a military commission, and shot on the spot. See that this is done immediately."

Before the overwhelming forces which Prince Repinn was manœuvring towards the central part of Prussia, and the openly hostile attitude of the Berliners in offering their hand to the Russians, Eugene found himself constrained to retreat from Berlin and put the Elbe between him and his innumerable adversaries. Disdaining personal success, he was not willing, at any price, to risk compromising, unless by the Emperor's orders, the last army in front of the enemy. But, deeply affected in his pride by this incessant retreat (happily this was the last step), he could not prevent a feeling, not of discouragement, but of sadness, overcoming him : —

SCHÖNEBERG, March 2, 1813.

Again another retrograde movement, my dear Augusta. I have decided to retreat to the Elbe, and I hope when I reach there to be more tranquil. I now have eight or ten thousand cavalry under arms. Of my own corps I have but eight or nine hundred. My infantry are also under arms constantly. All this maddens me ;

but there is no other way of doing. To-day is Mardi-gras, so they tell me. It has never passed so sadly before for us.

The Emperor, who from Paris was anxiously following the Viceroy's movements, reproached him with some bitterness for abandoning Berlin. Great as he was, Napoleon was not exempt from that weakness shown in the case of Masséna and Davout, of throwing upon the shoulders of his lieutenants the responsibilities of badly managed situations, for whose miscarriage he himself was first responsible. In reply to his criticisms, Eugene respectfully defended his manœuvres, imposed by the exigencies of the moment and the impossibility of struggling with nine hundred horses against an enemy's cavalry consisting of nine thousand horses. This defence he urges with all the marks of the deepest devotion and the greatest self-abnegation, emotions so honest in their expression that they could not fail to touch Napoleon's heart, — a heart weighed down with anguish at the critical position in which he stood.

March 15, 1813.

SIRE, — I can see by the last letters received from Your Majesty that you do not approve of any of the military dispositions which I took for the march to the

Elbe; and I also think you do not approve of the position which I thought it my duty to take upon the borders of the river. Obliged to regulate my conduct by the events around me, whilst I had great need of Your Majesty's directions, I did what I thought best for your service. I thought to follow the lessons of prudence, and not to go far out of the right path, in obeying the inspirations of my heart. The great interests inadvertently fallen into my hands demanded more talent than zeal, and were, perhaps, superior to all the efforts of my devotion. If, therefore, Your Majesty thinks, as your letters lead me to believe, that I have not fulfilled your views, I pray you not to leave me any longer in a position in which I can displease you, and I conjure you to replace me by some one more worthy as Commander-in-Chief of the army ; and, as it is far from being my desire not to serve you actively at this hour, I desire that Your Majesty give me a command in which I can still give proofs of my zeal and eternal attachment to Your Majesty.

Napoleon's character was of too high an order not to enable him to recognise his error in making unjust reproaches. Does not his laconic reply indicate his regret for his hasty judgment?

My Son, — I received your letter of March 15. The observations which I made on the different movements are for the good of the service, and you were wrong to give them any other interpretation.

In the mean while the Russians advanced in solid columns, slowly, it is true, for they awaited the moment — and but a few days separated them from it — when all the Prussian forces, exalted by the excitement of love of Fatherland, would march with them.

Eugene, after having concentrated all his reinforcements, found himself at the head of fifty thousand men, confronted by an enemy four times as strong. Such a disproportionate number, it can be easily understood, was a grave subject of uneasiness for him. His anxiety can be imagined when he received from Milan alarming news of his beloved wife's health. Traces of this anguish can be found in this letter : —

WITTENBERG, March 8, 1813, Morning.

On reaching here I was very much worried to learn, by the couriers of the 24th, that you had been taken ill so suddenly. Since then I know by your letter of the 25th that you are slightly better; but, in God's name, take good care of your precious health. I am in trouble enough, in being so far away from you, not to have the extra sorrow of knowing you are ill. In that case, I do not know if I should have the courage to remain here.

IV.

Events crowded fast upon one another. Napoleon, having hastily reorganised an army, announced his return. He had given the Prince orders to concentrate his forces at Magdeburg. On March 17th, Prussia cast aside her mask and declared war, as Eugene had foreseen for some time, and as Napoleon had expected, giving this expectation of his as a pretext of justification for the military preparations he had made on so grand a scale. Soon the French cannon thundered anew, no longer to retard the advancing enemy, but to oblige him to retreat in his turn.

The offensive once taken, all Eugene's confidence burst forth anew. His only thought was to prevent the Princess from worrying too much on his account.

MAGDEBURG, March 24, 1813.

I crossed the Elbe yesterday. With two divisions of infantry and one corps of cavalry we repulsed all the enemy's advance posts. To-morrow I hope to send them five or six leagues farther on. In this manner we shall draw near Berlin, and give the enemy a fair amount of annoyance. During this time the division forming the Army of the Rhine will arrive, and during the first fortnight in April we shall be in a fair way to begin hostilities. I hope you will be sensible enough not to worry yourself. If some threatening danger easily alarms your tenderness, you will find a consolation in knowing that I am doing my duty, and that I am happy in being able to prove useful to the Emperor, especially at a time and under circumstances when so many men have lost courage. I like to think that did I act otherwise you could no longer love or esteem me. A few more difficulties to combat, a little more patience, and, above all, confidence in my star.

In the following, by Darnay, we find one of those beautiful traits of devotion and personal valour with which this intrepid soldier-life is filled : —

" The day after this skirmish, the Viceroy with a large escort was reconnoitring the ground where he had fought the day before, when he was assailed by a body of Cossacks who had been in ambush. Several chasseurs of his escort were killed by sabre-strokes, among them the one who carried the Viceroy's portfolio. In the *mêlée*, Colonel Kliski, a Pole, who accompanied the Prince as ordnance officer, found himself surrounded by several Cossacks. The Viceroy, seeing the danger and embarrassment of the Colonel, ran to his succour, and dispersed his assailants by a few pistol-shots, putting them to flight. The dragoons of the Viceroy's escort recaptured the portfolio, slashed with sabre-strokes.

" I thought it my duty to give this particular incident

in detail, as it reflected so much honour on Prince
Eugene. The Viceroy, at the first appearance of danger
to one of his men, forgetting his title of Commander-in-
Chief, listened but to the promptings of his courageous
and generous heart. This noble trait was noised about
and repeated throughout the army, who, in their admiration for this noble devotion of the General to the soldier, cried out, ' There is a brave man, a friend to the
soldier ! ' Colonel Kliski every year, on the anniversary of the event, addressed a letter of thanks to his
Viceroy."

On April 5th, Eugene was attacked near Moe-
ckern by sixty thousand Russians and Prussians.
He held his own against them with his accustomed
bravery and vigour ; but did not judge it prudent to
risk a general battle with them at that time, especially as the Emperor was to come in person and
direct the manœuvres. He retreated in the night
to Magdeburg, and remained on the defensive.
Work, as Eugene puts it, did not diminish for his
army. The alliance of the Prussians with the
Russians brought the difficulties of his defensive
task to a climax, added to the fatigues of the
troops, and, above all, of their Commander-in-Chief,
who for so many months — since he left Italy, in
fact — had not enjoyed one day of real rest.

Learning that it was a question of appointing

his successor, he rejoiced at the idea of once more embracing the beings so unutterably dear to him, and from whom he had been so long separated; but he would not listen to the idea of giving up his command until after making the enemy feel at least once more the weight of his victorious arms. This compensation was due him after the awful retreat he had so worthily conducted.

In telling the Princess of these noble sentiments, he adds a few lines which are a new proof of his keen insight. They are about Fouché, whom Napoleon, before setting out for the Grand Army, had nominated a member of the Council of the Regency, and of whose future treason he seemed to feel a presentiment.

This view, in a way prophetic, appears still more remarkable when we know that Eugene had also expressed, in one of his letters to the Princess, a strong distrust of Marmont, when the latter was named a Marshal of the Empire after the battle of Wagram, — a mistrust which was about to be fulfilled the next year by the defection of the Commander of the Sixth Corps at Essonnes. These presentiments of the treason of two men elevated to the highest rank and overwhelmed with benefits by Napoleon, to whose downfall they contributed more than any one else, are they not convincing proofs of the honesty of his mind and the soundness of his judgment?

The Prince had passed through the fatigues of this long and hazardous campaign with remarkable endurance. It was time, however, for him to take some rest; but with what coolness and good-humour he speaks of the great fatigue which obliged him to keep his bed all day!

ASCHERLEBEN, April 14, 1813.

I hasten to assure you, my dear Augusta, I have tired myself out a good deal these last few days, and yesterday on dismounting I found I could not stand. I am in bed to-day, growling against my enforced rest, and with a very weak voice ; but all this is not dangerous, and I shall be entirely well in two days.

At last Eugene is on the eve of joining the great army, marching under Napoleon's orders. Again war is about to commence; but Eugene only sees the peace which will follow, and his return to the family fireside.

ASCHERLEBEN, April 25, 1813.

The moment has arrived for the reunion of the armies. Then we shall be very strong, and I shall be very happy to be rid of my heavy responsibility. I hope that the moment of our meeting is nearer than we think, for I am of the opinion that peace will be declared after the first victory. My health will be better when I am near you. This is the only wish left on this earth for me.

Napoleon had ordered Eugene to repair to Leipzig by the way of Magdeburg, whilst he advanced towards the same point by way of Lützen. As he entered Mersebourg, he heard a quick cannonade, and marching unhesitatingly to the spot from whence the salute came, he at last joined the Emperor near Gustavus Adolphus' monument. It was a happy augury.

IN CAMP NEAR LÜTZEN, May 2, 1813, 5 A. M.

I have been with the Emperor since yesterday evening at four o'clock. We had a little affray yesterday which would have been of no consequence to us, had not a bullet settled poor Marshal Bessières. I did not have one man wounded among my troops, and we captured a few prisoners. A remarkable thing happened. My reunion with the Grand Army was made precisely in front of the Gustavus Adolphus monument, on the anniversary of one of his battles. Adieu, my good Augusta. The Emperor received me with a great deal of kindness.

V.

Eugene took a prominent part in the battle of Lützen, and contributed largely to the victory, as much by his bravery as by his military genius. The day before, during his march towards Leipzig, he had manœuvred his columns in such a manner as to be able, according to circumstances, to direct them towards that city, or to bring them to Lützen, — tactics in which the pupil showed himself worthy of the master, and the lessons he had received in Napoleon's school.

On May 2d, the Viceroy had reached Leipzig when he received the order to return to Lützen. He retraced his steps rapidly, and by suddenly attacking the right flank of the enemy, menaced their only retreating bridges, and contributed in a large measure to their overthrow. Then he recaptured from the Allies several villages which they had succeeded in taking by concentrating all their forces, and the possession of which determined the fate of the day. Throwing himself upon the Prussians' right wing with as much good luck as rapidity and skill, he placed the enemy in so perilous a situation that notwithstanding old Blücher's impetuous passion and his desperate charges, the Allies were obliged to retreat.

As usual, it is with a charming modesty that he speaks or, better still, evades speaking of the part rightfully belonging to him in this victory, — the forerunner of the campaign of 1813.

BIVOUAC NEAR FORGAN, May 3, 1813, Evening.

Yesterday we fought a splendid battle, my dear Augusta; and, just as I said, it was all in our favour. The Russian and Prussian armies attacked us on our right whilst I was marching on Leipzig. We turned on them at once, and, notwithstanding their superiority in cavalry, we defeated them. The Emperor Alexander and the King of Prussia were present. A number were killed and wounded.

This battle of Lützen, which followed soon after that of Bautzen, might have given to Napoleon an advantageous peace, with the same fair conditions as that of Prague, assuring to France the frontiers of the Alps and the Rhine. It marked an important date in Eugene's life. It was, in fact, the last grand battle in which he took part under Napoleon's eyes, under whom he had never ceased to fight since his sixteenth year. But the Emperor needed him in Italy, where, before the end of this long campaign, the Prince was to render conspicuous services.

Before his departure he had the fortune to dis-
tinguish himself by pursuing the enemy, and inflict-
ing considerable loss among their soldiers, during
the following days. On May 5th, he had a lively
engagement with the Russians, whom he defeated
at Waldheim, after killing two thousand of their
men. The next day, as they were again trying
to hold their own before him, he treated them
more rudely still. Eugene gives but a few words
to the description of these different combats.

BEFORE WALDHEIM, May 6, 1813, 10 A. M.

MY DEAR AUGUSTA, — I am sitting in a little cabin
on my way to Dresden. Yesterday I had three different fights, — with the Eleventh Corps, with three Prussian divisions who tried to prevent me from crossing the
Mulda at Kolz, and, in the evening, with two divisions
of Russian grenadiers who were defending a superb
position. This was taken from them by our troops
with much daring. I think the Emperor will be satisfied, for the enemy's rout was complete.

Adieu, my dear friend; I am very well, and, at the
rate the Emperor is taking us, I hope to see you soon.

Always defeating the Russians, nearly always
on horseback at the head of his troops, and the
foremost in danger, the Viceroy found no time
during several days to correspond with the one
who awaited news of him with so much anxiety.

In ten days he was engaged in no fewer than five battles, from which he came out with as much honour as success.   At last, on May 8, near midday, he reached Dresden.   At daybreak the next day he left the city with the artillery of the Guard to reconstruct a pontoon bridge to which the Prussians had set fire; and he aided brilliantly in the manœuvres which forced the Allies finally to abandon the capital of Saxony, into which Napoleon desired to make a triumphant entry.   This was a happy but fleeting success, which cast a transient splendour over the last days of this campaign.

DRESDEN, May 10, 1813.

We reached here the day before yesterday, my dear Augusta.   I was at the head of the first troops.   I made a tour of the city to post the sentries and maintain order.   Afterwards I pursued the enemy, and forced him to burn the bridges which he had built near the city.   I did not take formal possession of it until in the afternoon.   I made my entry with the Emperor.   I had only written you a few days since the battle of the 2d, as I have been almost constantly on horseback. I had five victorious battles with the enemy, and each time we maintained our position.   Yesterday we worked at rebuilding a bridge under a lively fusillade; but we finished it this morning, notwithstanding our enemy's cannons.

At last Eugene received the order to return to
Italy! What joy filled his heart when Napoleon
announced these good tidings to him, — tidings
so long and anxiously looked for. Fate rewarded
the longings of the soldier and the husband.
He had not wished to leave the army without
one victory which should revenge at one and the
same time all the bitterness of the disastrous
defeat. Heaven had granted him Leipzig. He
could leave contentedly, and proud also of the
great services which for more than a year he had
rendered the Emperor and France. Those last
five months of retreat, above all, merited the
recognition of his country. Having received from
Murat's hands but a few thousand men, weakened,
disbanded, and completely demoralised, he had
succeeded, harassed by forces of crushing superiority, and across a hostile country, in conducting
one of the finest retreats in the annals of military
history, and which necessitated on his part an
energy and a prudence almost superhuman.
Better still, reorganising as he retreated, he
performed the miracle of transforming a handful
of disbanded soldiers, abandoned to him by the
King of Naples, into a well-organised corps of
eighty thousand men, whom he turned over to

Napoleon on the Elbe. Moreover, on leaving the army he was not to find repose in Italy, for according to the Emperor's orders he was to assume the heavy duty of raising one hundred thousand men capable of defending the kingdom against Austria, whose neutrality had taken upon itself an aspect altogether hostile.

It can be seen that in sending Josephine's son far from him, the Emperor intrusted him with a mission of great responsibility.

Eugene set out with a joyful heart at last to rejoin his beloved family. How long that separation had been, — more than a year! but painful as it had been, the glory which crowned Eugene's name, had it not compensated for all the sorrow?

Napoleon penned his order for departure with his usual military brevity : —

My Son, — Set out this evening by way of Munich to enter Italy. I have given orders to the Minister of War to place under your orders all my Italian and Illyrian troops.

Napoleon announced by courier Eugene's departure to the Princess. She, in communicating the news to Baron Darnay, cried out in the intoxication of happiness overflowing her heart: " I am at the very summit of my happiness! "